MW00412064

The people in Marla Cantrell's debut collection of southern short stories dream big, fall hard, and set the record straight. Each is like the story version of a country song. The common thread is that they're all set in Arkansas, during the four seasons of the year. Redemption happens on an icy day, spring brings rebellion, summer finds a woman reckoning with a choice she made years ago, and fall starts with a woman standing buck naked in the picture window of her house.

In the title story, "Early Morning in the Land of Dreams," a tough-as-nails woman breaks all the rules at her job at a call center, giving advice to the callers who've come to depend on her to get them through the night. "Calling Out the Moon" explores the breadth and width of friendship, particularly between two men who've known each other for more than sixty years. In "The Constitutional Rights of Gilly Lamproe," a convenience store clerk takes on The Man to prove she's every bit as good as anybody else—and a whole lot more fun. "A Million Shattered Stars" begins with a contentious relationship between a mother and her daughter and ends with fireworks everywhere. Glen Campbell shows up in "Remnants of Another Time," three days after his death, to save a woman whose life is crumbling.

Cantrell's voice is spare and complicated, a feat that's not easy to achieve, but one that makes these stories shimmer. The people she writes about live in small places, on land that means something to them. In this regard, the stories take on the additional meaning of place. This book couldn't be set anywhere else. It is a love letter to Arkansas.

Early Morning in the Land of Dreams

short stories

Marla Cantrell

Telephee
PRESS

This is a work of fiction. Names, characters, places, and incidents are either fictitious or used fictitiously. Any resemblance to an actual person (living or dead), places, or events is purely coincidental.

Telephee
PRESS

Print ISBN: 978-1-7357255-0-5
Copyright © 2020 Marla Cantrell
All rights reserved.

No part of this book may be reproduced in any form or by any electronic or mechanical means, including information storage and retrieval systems, without written permission from the author, except for the use of brief quotations in a book review.

Cover Design: Artifex 323 Design – Jessica Meadors
Interior Design: Rachel Snider

For Anita, who believed

WINTER

Afternoon of Ice and Stone 8

We Live for Yesterday, We Live for Tomorrow 14

A Thousand Floating Cranes 20

Broken Like Stone 27

On the Eve of the Eve of the End of the World 33

SPRING

The Constitutional Rights of Gilly Lamproe 40

Up on Piney Mountain 45

Carry Me Over 55

When the Lights Go On Again All Over the World 62

Early Morning in the Land of Dreams 68

Remnants of Another Time 78

SUMMER

A Million Shattered Stars 86

She Broke My Heart and Stole My Wallet 93

Sometimes You Forget 98

One Summer in Judsonia 104

Struck 111

Past the End of Everything 118

Calling Out the Moon 124

FALL

She'll Be Back 132

Rocket Men 139

Where the Tigers Sleep 146

As Long as You Remember 153

Mama Says She Loves Me, but She Lies 159

Landslide 166

Miss Maizie County's Public Disgrace 173

Afternoon of Ice and Stone

T-Buddy looked out the window above his narrow bed. Rain had turned to ice during the night, and now the limbs of his pecan tree appeared to be covered in glass. He knew one thing; he wouldn't be going in today. His own mama was killed on the highway, back when he was eleven, on her way to work on a day much like this one. He remembered it all: the cop showing up at his door asking for T-Buddy's daddy, who hadn't been around in seven years. He remembered the way the sleet pelted the porch and how he believed that if he let the officer come in, a great hole might form there in the living room and take T-Buddy down into it.

T-Buddy's boss at Hauling Class was none too happy when he took the call. "You're a delivery man," he said, and then he spelled the word d-e-l-i-v-e-r-y. "They ain't even letting schools out. If you can't make it in today, don't bother coming back."

He'd taken the job in the summer, when the only threats were heatstroke and bad drivers and road construction. None of that was enough to warn him away. He hadn't thought about winter.

That was the flaw in his nature, not seeing far enough down the road.

He looked around his house, so small he could pull it behind his pickup if he could force it from its foundation. It was perfect in its smallness: mini-fridge, a loveseat that filled an entire wall, a table that folded out in case he had company. He never did.

There was nothing to do but go back up to his loft where his single bed waited. He switched on the TV to the cooking network and watched skinny chefs make fat food so beautiful it looked like art. At noon, he opened a can of chili, slid a frozen blackberry pie into his tiny oven, and ate it all. There was no more food in the house.

T-Buddy had a pair of cleats from his football days. He put them on. He wrapped a red bath towel around his neck like a scarf. He put on his grandpa's old army jacket. He took a nerve pill and pocketed the bottle. The market was twelve blocks away, and he headed toward it.

The cleats were a bad idea, more like skates on the slick walk. Before he reached the end of his street, he'd moved onto the grass. He thought about the last time he'd worn the shoes. He'd been a tackle in high school. Out there, his body worked in his favor, his surprisingly quick gait, his strong legs, his chest like something you'd see on the cover of *Men's Health*. Football helped him deal with the loss of his mama back then, to hit another person and not get blamed for it. He pounded one gloved fist into his open palm. "Bam," he said aloud, and the word echoed in the still, blue air.

A car crept by, the first one he'd seen, and the driver waved. T-Buddy waved back and then stepped a little farther off the sidewalk. A car could skid, could swerve, before you had time to do much of anything. The nerve pills rattled in his pocket.

When he reached the intersection, he hit the "WALK" button, stepped back onto the brown grass, and waited. He looked down the street and saw a Hauling Class truck headed his way. The truck stopped at the traffic light, and T-Buddy turned his head away. It was too late. His friend Basil had seen him, and he was honking now and rolling down his window. "Because of you, I'll be working past midnight, man. What the hell?" Basil touched his temple. "You sick in the head or something?"

T-Buddy felt his stomach clench. A car behind Basil honked, and he waved the driver past. "Get over here, T-Buddy. Climb in and talk to me. I'll stay put." He looked T-Buddy up and down and waited.

Stepping into that truck was hard like fighting a battle is hard, like walking a tightrope is hard. Touching the bottle with his nerve pills helped. Still, he shook as he landed one cleat on the running board and hoisted himself up.

Before the door shut, Basil took off. T-Buddy gripped the dash and worked the seatbelt with his other hand. "You idiot," he said, but that only made Basil drive faster. There was a slick spot on Meadow Lake Road, and the truck fishtailed and T-Buddy cried out, and then he popped another one of his pills, swallowed it dry, wiped his brow.

"You got nerves like my aunt Edna," Basil said. And then he punched T-Buddy's arm. "We got a near perfect safety record. You can look it up. Roads are just roads, weather's just weather. Your time comes or it don't."

"That's what the preacher said about my mama." T-Buddy shook his head. "Didn't believe it. Didn't believe the rest of it either. Heaven and whatnot and streets of gold. She was only twenty-nine," he said, then turned his head to look out the passenger window.

The wind was howling. A tree branch popped and fell. "I had a sister die at seven," Basil said. "Seven. Made no sense at all, but there you go. I got a girl that's six now. Can't hardly look at her sometimes. I watch her sleep most nights. I take her to the doctor and make him check her out four times a year, blood work, scans, the whole nine yards. I do what I can, but it don't amount to much. That's just the way this world works. Fighting it is like fighting your own shadow."

T-Buddy couldn't take other peoples' sad stories. That's why he watched so many cooking shows. No sickness there. He looked down the stretch of highway. The power lines bounced in the wind. Two miles up ahead, around the bend, was where his mama's car caught air, where it sailed across the railroad tracks, where it upended in the ditch. He felt eleven again, motherless, and he wanted to feel ten or nine or even eight. At eight, the world was still a good place.

Pointing in the direction of his dead mama's wreck, he said, "I can't go up there."

Basil looked at him, opened his mouth to say something, paused, and then reconsidered. "We can circle around. I got a delivery up on Old Vega Road anyway."

The road they turned onto was gravel, the kind where there's always a lone dog scruffing around, where there's always a line of fence posts half eaten away by rot. The truck slipped on the turn, and then straightened out, and then stopped cold. T-Buddy squeezed his eyes shut, tried to breathe.

"Well, looky there," Basil said, and T-Buddy opened his eyes. In a field were three sculptures made of cement and all kinds of junk: wire, pieces of broken bottles, green and blue and brown, and round mirrors that caught reflections of the clouds and threw them back.

"What the heck?" T-Buddy said, and then he pointed. "That one up by the old barn, that's an angel, right? You see an angel?" He got out of the truck and crunched along the gravel, then slipped through the fence, and headed toward it. Basil followed, stopping at the concrete cow with a wine bottle for a tail, an old antenna on its shoulders like wings.

T-Buddy glanced at the statue that looked like a life-size Volkswagen, a giant pink peace sign on the driver's door. A real steering wheel sat on the hood, making it look as if you could wind it up and drive it away.

Moles and armadillos and gophers had done their work on the pasture, the ground was tunneled and fell with T-Buddy's footfalls. He stumbled, got back up, walked faster. The angel, whose wings were iridescent things, seemed to call his name. The angel's hair, a red wig that had been dipped in shellac, fanned out as if a strong wind were blowing. He stood and took her in, her chicken wire skirt, her blue marble eyes, her hands two icy garden trowels.

Behind him, Basil climbed atop the cow, slipped across its icy back, and smiled. Then he took out his phone and snapped a photo of himself. At the same time, T-Buddy reached out his hand and touched the frozen chicken wire on the angel, the trowels. He started to reach up to touch her wings, but something stopped him. There was too much beauty in them, maybe that was it, or it might have been that they seemed so delicate they might turn to powder. So he stood there with his hand raised, and the sun broke from behind a cloud, and a covey of bobwhites rose and flew over him.

On the last night of his mama's life, she was wearing a black T-shirt that read "Keep on Truckin'" and pink sweatpants, and when she said goodnight, she stood at his bedroom door for a long time, framed in light, so that she seemed to glow when he turned in his bed and saw her still there. For a moment, he had this thought: she looks like an angel. And as he fell asleep, he imagined her, her red hair let down from its ponytail, flighty wings suddenly appearing where her shoulder blades should have been.

Once, she told him her idea of heaven was twenty acres and a good barn, a cow named Miss Priss, and him. "Nothing else I'd need," she'd said, and he'd not even looked up when she said it, that's how unimportant it seemed at the time. She might have wondered if he'd heard her, if he'd remember how carefully she had loved him, once he was grown. T-Buddy shaded his eyes and looked at the angel's stone face, and he wondered who had made her, or if she'd fallen in this field from on high, just for him. The thought made everything that hurt in him bust free. He breathed in deep, and it felt as if there was suddenly more room in his chest. He touched the open spot with his gloved fingers. It ached still, that tender place did, but not nearly as much as it had before.

We Live for Yesterday, We Live for Tomorrow

Me and my old lover Hollis are bundled up and sitting on his front porch, and we're listening to the old stuff –Patsy Cline, Roy Acuff, Johnny Cash, Eddie Arnold, Kitty Wells—and we're comparing them to some of the new singers, guys and gals about as sincere as Hollywood and twice as pretty. All their Botoxed faces smooth like a month-old concrete sidewalk, even the country stars older than we are.

Hollis shakes his head, rubs his beard, and says, "They don't hold a candle." And then, butted right up against that sentence, he says, "You remember when Mama and Daddy danced right over there under that tree?" and this is where he takes his cigarette and points to the pecan tree that's so tall it blocks out the sun when it's leafed out proper, which it would be if it wasn't December.

"I remember it all," I say, and that's when Roy Acuff starts singing "Tennessee Waltz," and the fiddle kind of reaches out and grabs both of us, and Hollis grips the porch railing to steady himself, and I grab hold of the arms of the rocking chair and close my eyes.

"They cut quite a rug," Hollis says. And then, as if I didn't know exactly who he meant, he says, "My mama and daddy did. When they danced, it seemed like they was taking their vows all over again."

"The first time I saw them dance was when I realized what a beauty your mama was. I was only fifteen then, and already so in love with you I couldn't see good," I say, and Hollis bows his head so I can't see his face at all.

"You're still pretty as a shined-up pickup, Jubilee," he says.

"Maybe thirty years ago I didn't look so bad," I say. "Maybe before I got knocked around by love and whatnot and lost my mind."

Hollis looks off to the north, to the lights of the nearest town that sits at the tip-end of Arkansas.

"We all lose our minds eventually," he says, "even Mama at the end when we had to put her in the home. Daddy would sit with her every day."

"It's why you can't love nobody," I say. "You got a inflated view of what love looks like." We'd brought the eggnog out with us, and I'd dumped half a bottle of bourbon into it. I take a sip, and the fire burns and then spreads the way a good fire does.

Hollis grabs his coffee cup and dunks it in the punchbowl. The eggnog drips off the side and onto his boots. "I loved you plenty back when we were going out," he says and waves the smoke from in front of his face.

"You loved me about as good as you could," I say. "It's not the same thing."

15

Just then, Johnny Cash starts singing "I Walk the Line," and the tempo picks up. Hollis lights another cigarette from the red end of the one that's expiring. He says, "Water under the bridge, Jubilee. Water under..." and then he just stops.

Earlier today I was sitting out here, coat on, mittens on, and a swarm of starlings flew over. They moved like a person double-jointed, like a ballerina, the flock of them swaying across the sky, making patterns that looked like a hornet's nest and then a fishing net and then a giant diamond.

I look over at Hollis, and he's gone away inside his head like he does when he hears something he don't want to hear. "We stayed friends, though," I say. "Not a lot of people can say that."

"I've known you since before we both could walk," he says. "I'll probably know you when we both can't walk again."

"Call me a fool," I say, "but I think a walk right now would do us both good."

"It's nigh on midnight, girl."

"You got someplace else to be?"

It is harder to walk at night than I remembered. Even with the moon, even with the flashlight, me and Hollis bump into each another, we hit a fencepost by the south pasture, we snag our jeans on the barbed wire. But once we're out in the field, we do a little better. There are sounds at night, hoots and hollers and dogs and grass rustling, and rumbling from the highway not so far away. The grass has gone fallow, turned gold and stiff, and it crunches beneath our boots. The cold is making my eyes water, making my nose water, filling my lungs with air that stings.

When we get to the stack of square hay bales that should be in the barn but aren't, we climb up and sit side by side under the chalkboard sky. Hollis is breathing hard, he's wiping his brow in this cold night, and I've got a pain that's riding my side, but I don't act like it.

"You ought to stop smoking," I say to Hollis, and he puts his cigarette back in the pack.

"No place to do it," he says, "except a clinic in hell-fire Minnesota. You believe that?" he asks. "It's probably thirty below right now. If that's not a place where a little smoke and fire would help, I don't know where is. It's like a cosmic joke, but nobody else seems to understand that."

"So, you looked into it?"

"Got a brochure back at the house. Daddy had the emphysema. I don't want that."

"My mama had that shaking disease," I say. "Daddy didn't stay around long enough for us to know what he had."

The night is littered with glittered stars. Hollis is the only warmth around, and so I scoot closer. The eggnog is still working its magic, and I feel like I could levitate if I tried.

"What was your parents' secret?" I ask, and Hollis opens his mouth to speak and then stops. I take my mittens off so I can feel the hay. I like the way it smells, how it seems to take all of summer and presses it into a tied-up thing.

"I think he liked taking care of Mama," he says finally. "She always seemed like a kid, even to me, which is why it was fun to grow up around her. She didn't like chores. She didn't like cooking, but she loved climbing trees. She loved fishing. Daddy liked to sit her down and help her write out a budget every month, and she never once that I know of stayed on it, so he was always playing catch up at Mina's Grocery, and Billie Joe's Dress Shop, and anywhere else she had a tab. As for Mama, I think she loved him most because he wasn't a liar and a cheat like her own daddy was. That, and he played the fiddle."

I like the way Hollis smells, like chimney smoke and cigarette smoke and Dial soap. I thought about the men I'd known after Hollis and I split up and I high-tailed it out of town, the low quality of every one of them when you got right down to it. "I never had one man wanted to do more than take the trash out," I say, and saying it makes my throat close because it's true and because I'm getting old.

Walking back across the pasture, we spot a coyote a few yards away, its eyes flashing, and Hollis takes his arm and moves me behind him. The coyote looks at us, sniffs the air, paces in a circle, and Hollis stands his ground long enough for the varmint to run off.

"I forgot what living in the country was like after I moved away," I say. "I seen a lot of things, most of them not worth telling, but this one time in Dallas a guy put on a flying suit that had red wings stitched to the back and swung himself off the bridge, and he floated down to the water where a boat was idling, ready to take him to shore."

"He didn't get hurt?"

"Nah," I say, "he got arrested."

"I never lived anywhere else," Hollis says. "Too much family here. Too much land in our name."

"You didn't miss a heck of a lot," I say, but the truth is he did.

Hollis holds the barbed wire with two gloved fists, opening it so I can crawl through, and then he walks ahead of me. Soon we're close enough to see the porch light. We'd left the music on, and Eddie Arnold is singing "Make the World Go Away."

I know it before he does, that he's going to dance. I know it because he's moving his feet like he's practicing, and then he

18

holds out his arms like there's a lady inside them, and he starts to sway back and forth, he starts to shuffle—there's no better word for it—and turn. When he gets to me, he stops like that, hands held out, the music like an ache from long ago. I look around, for who, I don't know, maybe the past, maybe his mama and daddy dancing like movie stars under the pecan tree. But nobody's there but me and Hollis, and I step into his circle, I let him hold me, and all the sounds of the night quicken and then flare and then go out, so that all that's left is us and the music and this one cold night.

A Thousand Floating Cranes

The Arkansas River, at least where Liddie lives, is not the world's most beautiful waterway, but she still goes to the grounds of the National Historic Site in Fort Smith to see it when the weather's nice. There's a spot where you can sit and watch the water churning below, where you can see the power of the river, the power of anything that bands together the way this water does, millions of drops gathered in this one place.

Today is cold, the sky burdened with clouds. Christmas was just three weeks ago, with its sugar cookies and spiked punch, and Liddie took as much as she could of it, knowing January was headed her way.

She has friends born in January. All of them are headstrong and beautiful. All of them seem to know the right thing to do, all the time. Not Liddie. She is rarely sure. All she knows today is that she doesn't want to go home.

So she drives instead. She scoots through Barling, then takes her SUV across the River Bottoms where the road curves, a graceful belly dancer covered in blacktop. She crosses the bridge, notices this section of the Arkansas River that slaps against the lock and dam. She had a high school friend drown not far from there, fifteen years ago. She can still see his face, his hair more red than brown. Bruce. Twenty-one when he died. She can still see him copying her answers in their sophomore science class. In all living things, the basic unit of life is the ____.

The answer is cell. Just one and you don't have much. Add thirty-seven trillion and you could make a person.

The road takes her to Van Buren, and she heads downtown. There's a bookshop across from the depot she adores. Chapters on Main. They sell the best coffee. She steps inside, orders her drink, browses the shelves.

At the end of Main Street, the Arkansas River shows up again. She used to go there as a kid and stand on the dock. A school of carp crowded the shore, waited for breadcrumbs and crackers that visitors brought as often as the sun came up. She remembers the fishes' smart silvery bodies, jumping from the water to grab the food. Maybe school is not the right word. She smiles at her cleverness. A university of carp, she thinks. That's more accurate.

Once, when she was eleven, she snatched communion wafers from her church's pantry to feed the fish. She's never gotten over it. That awful theft. That sacrilege. "Well," she says aloud. "You can't go back."

There's a woman browsing the shelves nearby. She is easily seventy years old. She is dressed in a long denim skirt, thick brown socks, fur-lined boots. She has more rings than fingers. She has silver hair that tumbles across her shoulders. She wears red lipstick and fake eyelashes and turquoise beads.

The woman steps closer, puts two fingers behind her ear. "Excuse me?"

Liddie, startled, says, "Sorry! Just talking to myself."

The woman holds out her hand, "CJ," she says, as a form of introduction. "Nice to meet you. And no worries about talking to yourself. All the best people do."

The two women talk books. They both love Joan Didion, Elizabeth Berg, Liane Moriarty, Barbara Kingsolver. They disagree on David Sedaris and John Grisham.

When Liddie's coffee is ready, the women sit together at one of the tables. A sound system pumps in smooth jazz, the smell of coffee a shawl around them.

"I've never met anyone who reads that I didn't like," CJ says. "They seem to be able to describe what they're feeling, which is a highly underrated skill."

When Liddie was a senior in high school, she went to hear a poet read. Her voice was like CJ's, all bells and flutes and enunciated words. Liddie fell under her spell. When the reading was over, she couldn't tell you one line the poet recited, yet she felt as if she understood every stanza.

She considers CJ's comment about feelings. "I've been feeling like I don't want to go home," Liddie says.

"Why is that?"

Liddie looks at her coffee. "My husband left me the first week of October. And then he came back at Christmas."

Liddie holds up her right hand and shows the diamond ring that sparkles on her finger. "He bought me this," she says.

"My," CJ says, "such a lovely trinket."

"Right. I mean about it being a trinket. Anyway, he's not the same. He wears this new cologne that has undertones of black pepper, I'm not even kidding, and I think, Who bought you that?"

"But he came home to you, Liddie."

"I know, and I should feel like I won a prize, right?" Liddie looks around and then leans in. "But I don't."

CJ wraps her fingers around her cup. "My ex-husband's name is Robert, but I called him Robbie. My rightful name is Clara Jane, but he called me CJ. We lived in a two-story house in the Historic District in Fort Smith." She shakes her head. "The work those old houses take to keep them standing. But we loved it, every sloping floor and rattling pipe. We poured our money into it, like cream into coffee.

"It wore us down after a while. And then it tore us down. Robbie lives in Muskogee now, in a modern house that doesn't demand a thing from him, with a woman who, as I understand it, demands everything."

"And your old house?"

CJ laughs. "It's a lawyer's office now. A divorce attorney!"

The front door opens, a little bell ringing when it does. A youngish woman, not too much older than Liddie, walks in with three little ones tagging behind. The youngest child, a girl in a red velvet coat, wipes her nose with her white mitten.

"Where do you live now?" Liddie asks, and CJ tells her she has an apartment a few blocks away.

CJ's face brightens, and she claps her hands. "Come see it!" she says.

CJ's apartment smells like patchouli and just-baked bread. Silk scarves drape the lamps in the small living room, and bookshelves line the walls. There is a sign above the kitchen table that reads, "Earth's Crammed with Heaven." And in the china hutch, tiny origami cranes rest, made from bits of wrapping paper, so many it's impossible to count.

"What's the deal with the cranes?" Liddie asks, and CJ tells her the Japanese legend. How you fold a thousand for yourself or someone with a desperate need. "They make wishes come true," she says, her chin raised, as if she's expecting Liddie to refute the claim.

Liddie looks at the older woman's knobby fingers, wondering how she's able to make those intricate folds, over and over again.

"What's your wish?" Liddie asks, and CJ says, "These aren't for me. I've been waiting for the right person to give them to. And today I decided. These are yours. All you have to do is tell me what you want."

Before Liddie can say a word, CJ goes to the kitchen to make lunch. There's something healing about having someone cook for you, and Liddie sits in the velvet chair in the living room, listening to CJ work.

After the asparagus soup and grilled cheese sandwiches are ready, Liddie learns that each crane takes CJ about five minutes. Liddie thinks, Five minutes times a thousand. Such a lot of time.

CJ breaks Liddie's concentration. "So," she says, "what's your wish?"

Liddie realizes that her husband hasn't asked her that question in a long time. Not when he moved out, and not when he moved back in. "I don't know. A say in how my own life turns out, maybe. A little bit of control over my future."

CJ listens, mentioning three books that might help. And then she says, "Sorry about the recommendations. Kind of a habit. You read so much, you think you can solve all the world's problems. But this is about you and the cranes. If you want to take your life back, then that's your wish."

Liddie's pulse quickens. "What happens now?"

CJ says, "Well, you could take the cranes home, spread them across your house. Or, you could release them. Some people let them float away in a stream or lake."

"Or a river?"

"Sure," CJ says. "Why not?"

The Arkansas River is only a few blocks from where they are now. They gather the cranes in grocery sacks and head out. Liddie holds CJ's arm when they get near the water, leading her down the slope to the soggy bank. A light mist is falling, and the sun is nowhere in sight.

Liddie kneels on the wet ground. She takes a handful of the cranes, some glossy pink, some made of Christmas paper, some a small violet print, and drops them in the water. They bob on the surface, they float and float, as Liddie scoops up more of the birds and lets them fall.

They look like little flowers on the surface of the water. Liddie thinks about the night her husband left, how she blocked the bedroom door and wailed as he moved her aside and walked past her. Her cheeks burn at the thought.

And then she thinks of her old friend Bruce. The last day she saw him, she'd been working at the Sonic, just yards from where she is now. When she'd taken him his food, he'd told her he'd just gotten a job at the Housing Authority, patching up empty apartments. He said, "I freakin' love my life."

Liddie wants to love her life. Wants to wake up eager to see what the day will bring. She stands up straighter, watches the thousand cranes ride the choppy water.

CJ has made her way to Liddie's side, and she slips her arm around Liddie's waist. The grocery bags are empty now, and the cranes are now beginning to sink. "My university of cranes,"

Liddie says.

"Your university of cranes," CJ repeats. "Oh, how I love that."

In the weeks to come, Liddie will move her husband into the guest bedroom. She will take a hammer to his bottle of cologne, and he will never ask where it went. She will change her hair, her diet, her daily routine. She will start a book club with CJ. She will start taking yoga, will read books about meditation. Will start folding cranes.

Her husband will feel the churning of a man suddenly unsure of his life. He will stand up to Liddie, only once, and lose. He will go sullen and realize his sullenness is unnoticed. By spring, he'll realize he only wants to stand in Liddie's wonder for as long as he can. For she radiates light as well as the sun. She is his everything.

It is a shame that this realization has come too late.

Broken Like Stone

The rock fell. That was all Cookie Whittington knew. It fell
from a bridge to the silver Buick below. The Buick that held her
Vernon. He was coming to get her. She had called. Distraught.
Over the new exercise class that promised to make her look
twenty again. How stupid it seemed now, the way she cried in
the parking lot, covered in sweat, her hair soaked, her T-shirt
straining against her belly. She'd only made it through ten
minutes of the class. The rest of the women were gazelles,
whippets, or possibly drug addicts by the way they ran and
jumped and screamed encouragement at eight o'clock in the
morning. The blonde in the red sports bra kept clapping her
hands, yelling, "You can do it! You can do it!"

It was obvious Cookie could not. She felt as if she might die.
Defeated, she raised her hand for a bathroom break and trotted
out of the gym, not even stopping to put on her coat. In the car,
she ran her hands over her squishy thighs. She'd had dreams
once: her body like a supermodel's, the long line of her sculpted
legs peeking through an open trench coat, her waist so small it

looked as if she might snap in two.

But that was not who Cookie was now. She was a thirty-seven-year-old fatty who'd been steeped in queso from the local Mexican joint, filled with root beer from the town's one drive-in, flush with frozen coconut cake she ate from the box she bought weekly at the discount grocery store.

And so she called Vernon. She wept great tears as if someone had died when really she had only awakened to her true self. "Come get me," she said. "I don't think I can drive." Just like that Vernon left his cubicle at Ashworth Tile where he'd been hunched over his desk, figuring out how much grout it would take to rework old Mrs. Bondurant's downstairs shower. Cookie could see him pulling his blue plaid scarf from his coat pocket. She could see the slant of his shoulders as he headed for his car and the way his slick shoes slid on the circle of ice that had been a puddle just the day before.

In Hobbtown, there is a road that ducks under a stone bridge built in 1933. Vernon drove under it, and one of the stones fell and crashed through his windshield. Why the rock dislodged just at that time, no one knew. But they would investigate. They would surely investigate! Even hearing this was not enough to prepare Cookie for what came next. For even then, with her phone pressed against her ear, she imagined the rock to be small, the hole in the windshield fixable, her husband stunned but not eternally damaged.

But now she is sitting in a chapel inside Pleasant Hill Hospital with a priest and a rabbi, and she covers her mouth to stop the laughter that always comes when she is nervous. A priest and a rabbi, it sounds like the beginning of a joke. They stare at their feet, and then they tell her Vernon is dead. The rabbi says "passed," the priest says, "gone to his great reward." But they both mean dead.

Cookie wipes her brow. Her mouth goes dry. Her stomach jumps. She is shaking, visibly; the water inside the cup she's been handed is a tsunami. The holy men want her to identify Vernon, but she stalls. They will go with her, one or both—her decision— but instead, she closes her eyes and refuses to open them again. "Call my mom," she finally says. "She'll know what to do." She is suddenly fifteen again, a ward of her mother's again, unafraid to say she cannot or will not do what is necessary.

When her mother comes, they take the elevator down to the basement. They pass the cafeteria. The cooks are baking cinnamon rolls, the smell like a soft blanket that shields her from the cold, and for the first time in her life, she does not turn toward them. She walks past the clattering trays, the visitors sitting at stunted plastic tables, and she says aloud, "Who puts a cafeteria on the same floor as the morgue?"

Inside the morgue, on a table covered in marble, is her Vernon. She can tell by the wedding ring that bites into his finger. His hand has been placed on top of a white sheet, and Cookie looks no farther than his lonely wrist.

She is wearing her exercise T-shirt with the slogan that reads, "If I Can Get Through This I Can Get Through Anything." She crosses her arms to try to hide the words. It is as if a cruel prankster has written the script for this entire wretched day. She glances at her mother, who has willed herself to look at Vernon's face and is now paying for it.

The fluorescent light stutters for a second, turns to gray, then sputters back to life. Cookie finds the door, and then the bathroom, and finally the tile floor, where she plans to stay until someone bigger than she comes to take her away. And who, she thinks, is bigger than she is?

This is where her mother finds her. This is where her mother sinks to the floor beside her, dropping her handbag that slides three feet away. Crawling, she retrieves it, reaches in, fishes for the amber bottle. "Adderall," she says, and pulls out two pills, taking one and handing the other over. "It'll make the next few hours easier." When Cookie hesitates, her mother says, "I promise."

At most times, the size of your individual parts matters, but there are brief snippets when they do not. Cookie lets her stomach go slack. She slumps against the wall and seems to puddle there. A nurse comes in, looks around, backs away. Cookie and her mom are a sight right now. They are covered in their grief: hollowed-eyed, knees tucked to their chests, tears rolling like a river. When Cookie finally speaks, she says, "I killed Vernon. He was coming to get me, a grown woman, because I said I couldn't drive home from my exercise class. Because I was upset over my big behind. Because I was crying over my ruined body."

Her mother shakes her head. She takes Cookie's hand. "Our days are numbered from the time we're born. You couldn't have stopped today no matter what. We show up on this earth, we muddle through, and one day we're called to our eternal home. It's all laid out before we draw one breath."

Cookie wants to believe it's not her fault. She tries to imagine Vernon in heaven, but all she can see is him in a nicer cubicle. The monitor on his computer is gold trimmed, and he has wings, but nothing else has changed. Old Mrs. Bondurant still needs grout.

She remembers a day last summer when she and Vernon were stretched out in their double hammock. He was touching her shoulders, telling her how beautiful she was. She didn't feel beautiful and had not since she'd packed on twenty extra pounds that seemed to come out of nowhere.

"You are so wonderfully and beautifully made," he said, and she swatted his hand away. "Is that Shakespeare?" she asked, and he said, "That's King James."

"I don't think it was written for me," Cookie said, and Vernon said, "Of course it was."

My God, how she misses him.

"What am I supposed to do now?" Cookie asks.

Her mother mistakes the question, thinking Cookie is asking for an immediate plan. "There's no rule book, baby girl. When your daddy died, I started calling. I had my address book, and I went down the list. I even phoned our plumber. I said, 'From now on, I'll be handling the bills because Alton just expired.' The plumber was a kind man, and he said, 'I'll write that down, Mrs. Dupree. Your husband was a fine man, paid on time, liked to keep his pipes clean. I always appreciated that.'

"I liked what he said. Your daddy did like to keep the house up. And he did pay on time, which shows great character. Mostly, though, folks will say the wrong thing. They'll tell you to be thankful you had Vernon as long as you did. They'll tell you you're lucky because you had a man that didn't sneak around or ruin your credit. That'll come mostly from the divorcees. People will come up to you in the grocery store and ask if you're getting life insurance money. Then they'll ask you how much.

"None of that matters, though. The important part is to keep letting people talk. They want to help, by and large, they want to take a piece of your grief and carry it for you for a little while. That's the great mystery of people. Even when they say the worst wrong thing, they're trying."

In the hour or so that follows, Cookie lays with her head in her mother's lap. Already, her thighs are aching from the exercise class. There is a stain on the ceiling in the shape of Texas, and Cookie studies it, and cries until her throat hurts.

There is no way to judge time in a hospital basement, no sunlight sifting through open windows, no clouds to roll past. Cookie does not know how long she's been there until her mother shifts her weight and looks at her watch. "I think we should go," she says, and they pull themselves up, using each other and the wall to help them.

Neither is in any shape to drive, so they call a cab. They arrive at Cookie's house just as the sun is dipping so low in the sky it looks like a memory. Already, there are sympathy cards clipped to the screen door, and two cherry pies are sitting in a cardboard box on the porch. Cookie touches the card in the pink envelope and then takes each of them from the screen.

As she turns the key in the lock, she imagines her sweet Vernon on the other side of the door, his eyes as soft as starlight when he sees her. She can almost feel his hands as he runs them along her sides, loving every ounce of her. She shuts her eyes against the broken day, against her poor opinion of herself, against the hard days that follow. When she gets inside, she will look at her unmade bed, see Vernon's socks beside it. She will remember this always, the bedsheets rumpled, the last sign of her husband's life discarded on the carpet, tossed aside so easily in the early light of morning. So precious now in the deep, dark night.

On the Eve of the Eve of the End of the World

I'm sitting on the shoulder of the highway, two days before the end of the world. I slipped a Xanax in Loyal's soup at supper or I'd be in the storm cellar with him, stacking sacks of pinto beans onto the shelves we put in this summer.

Loyal and I live off a straight stretch of country road, by a white church that's been here since 1901. There are a lot of speeders that zip by here, in a hurry to get someplace else.

I've always liked watching cars go by. When I was a girl, my brother and I used to play a game where we'd guess the make and model of a car just by the sound of the engine as it topped the hill and then slipped down into the valley where we lived. We'd stand side by side and wait for them to get close enough for us to see. I almost never won.

The biggest win in my life is Loyal. I met him two weeks after Sid Preston broke up with me. I was a wreck, but Loyal kept telling me I was wonderful. After a while I started to believe him.

Sid's the mayor of Halfway now. He's caught up in a scandal because he put his girlfriend on the payroll and his wife found out. And then the news caught wind of it and interviewed the girlfriend, who looks like me twenty years and ten pounds ago. Blond hair to her waist, green eyes, a little top heavy.

They asked the girlfriend what she'd learned from her disgrace, and she said, "A lot. For instance, my grammar's better. The mayor taught me how to use 'seen' and 'saw' properly. For example, I'd never say, 'I seen Mayor Hawkins slipping tax money into a sack he took directly to his safety deposit box down at City Bank.' No sir, I know better now."

I think about what Sid taught me. I couldn't repeat any of it on TV.

Sid was a party waiting to happen, and he knew everybody. You'd go to a restaurant and you couldn't eat for the people coming over to say hi. With Loyal, it's different. He's a solitary man who likes the country, doesn't trust the government, and thinks the world is ending on Friday.

You probably wonder if I think the same. The short answer is no. But when all this started, Loyal and I were drifting a little. He works the graveyard shift at the steel plant, and I work days at a law office in town. On weekends, when we'd go for a drive, we couldn't talk for more than five minutes. I thought I might lose him, and then he heard a radio program about the Mayan calendar, which started five thousand one hundred and twenty-five years ago and stops cold on December 21.

"Only the strong and the true will survive," Loyal said. "I believe an asteroid will hit the earth, or something will happen with black holes in space. Either way, we need to get ready."

And then he said this: "You do believe I'm strong and true.

34

Don't you, Leigh?"

That broke my heart.

We spent days talking, figuring out how to get ready. He asked if I'd be willing to use some of our savings to deck out the storm cellar, and I said yes.

And then one day in the spring, I saw him unload his truck. He had eighteen jumbo packs of disposable diapers he'd bought from Sam's Club and was taking them into the cellar. We've been trying for a baby for three years now, and nothing, not even one false alarm.

I watched through the screen door and I imagined Loyal and me hunkered down underground and him pushing our two Army cots together and us finally making it happen.

That's why I go along with him. Even though I figure some Mayan just got sick of recording time, the way I get sick of my own job, when the big wigs down at the firm snap orders like I'm a fast-order cook and turn on their heels to take a three-hour lunch.

So sometimes I forget just how real this all is to Loyal. Three weeks ago, I made the mistake of asking Loyal what he wanted for Christmas. He put his hand on my shoulder and said, "Honey, nobody's celebrating Christmas this year. You've got to give up your old way of thinking."

We do have a Christmas tree in the living room. Loyal says it's better if we keep up appearances. He figures the fewer people who know what we're doing, the safer we'll be when folks have exhausted all the supplies in the Walmarts and Quick Piks and migrate to the country looking for food.

A car is coming. From the sound of the engine, I believe it's an SUV or a pickup. Like I said, I've never been too good at this game. I stand up and move back off the shoulder. As it gets closer, I can hear something else. "Santa Baby" is playing so loud it sounds like I'm in the good seats at a concert, and I realize the driver must have a speaker system on the outside of the car.

The SUV is covered with Christmas lights. There is a lighted wreath on the front grill.

The driver slows to a crawl. He rolls down the windows and shouts, "Merry Christmas!" Beside him is a woman, dark haired and smiling.

In the back, a boy, four or five years old, sticks out his stockinged head. His face is awash in the light from the car, and he looks otherworldly, like an angel sent down.

They look painfully happy, like actors selling toothpaste. I flash my best smile and wave at them as they pass. I want them to keep all their happiness. I want a world of happiness to descend on their car and ride through the world with them.

Tomorrow, Loyal wants to go into town and get matching tattoos that read, "Loyal and Leigh Mankin, Married 3-24-2006. May we never part."

I don't believe in marking my body. But I'll go just the same. I've spent the last year doing things I didn't believe in, just so I could stay close to Loyal. If the tattoos make him happy, so be it.

I head for home, bending to dip through the barbed wire fence. It's been too warm a year, and still my antique roses bloom.

I stop near the pond, the moon reflecting on its surface, and look up into the navy blue sky. I try to see this place the way Loyal must, a beautiful, doomed oasis.

A shooting star swooshes across the sky, flaring above me. Just then, another star whips by, and then another. I count ten in less than thirty seconds, more than I've ever seen, even in an entire night.

I stare at the sky. It has turned orange in spots. In others, light flashes white. The ground is shaking, and thunder—or what I think is thunder—roars, a lion capturing its prey.

My chest tightens. What if Loyal is right? What if this is the end of everything? I run, past the barn and the pond, past the grapevines that tangle near the fencerow. The sky is growing brighter, with hundreds of shooting stars that sweep and arc and then turn to nothing.

I stop, my breathing raspy, and squeeze my eyes shut. Should I try to make it back to the barn or sprint the quarter mile home? It's too much, and I'm shaking more than I ever have. I can feel my toes tremble inside my boots. Just then I see the porch light flicker on, the glow yellow on this troubled night. Somehow Loyal has awakened, pushed his way through the Xanax and found me missing. I run even faster, aiming for Loyal, who is strong and true, and who will know what to do, who has always known exactly what to do.

Spring

The Constitutional Rights of Gilly Lamproe

I look like Penelope Cruz if Penelope was blond and weighed twice as much as she does on her worst day. It gets me a lot of attention, especially when I wear fancy clothes, like the kind you see Penelope wear all the time, little wrap dresses and heels so high you could fall off them. Add a limp from a pedicure gone terribly wrong, and we could pass for sisters. But here's where we part ways. While she's feisty and sexy, I'm considered confrontational and inappropriate, at least that's what my latest performance review says.

Like I care what the folks at the Stop and Swap think. Ever since they got all highfalutin', adding cappuccino to the drink machines and making us wear red polyester dresses as uniforms, it's gone to H-E-L-L. And yeah, I say that out loud, sometimes when customers are around, so I guess that's where the confrontational thing comes in.

Everett, my boss, sat across the counter from me, a plate of nachos between us, and went over the whole thing. I got good grades for hygiene. I wash my hands real good. Tip: sing the ABC song, all the way through, out loud, so you don't forget any parts. And yeah, I do that, about thirty times a day, which I reckon could bother some folks.

Everett pointed to the section titled Personal Conduct. "The problems start here, Gilly," he said, "the sound of your voice is, uh, distinctive, so when you're on break, on the phone, talking to your boyfriend, saying things nobody else wants to hear, the rest of the staff can't not listen. I have your reprimand here, which I expect you to sign before this meeting is over, so we can put this behind us and move on to bigger and better things."

Everett, to his credit, blushed.

"We had a complaint from a co-worker, who requested to remain anonymous, so don't even ask," Everett said, and then he began to read. "The complainant reported that Gilly Lamproe, while on a company-owned phone, proceeded to describe events that transpired between herself and a man she called Hoss, which involved a motorcycle, a bottle of tequila, and an act deemed illegal in at least three Southern states."

I laughed. Somebody else might have denied it all, but I don't think telling the man you love what you plan to do to him the next time you meet should be against the law. "Shit and Shinola, Everett, riding a horse on Sunday is against the law over in Newton County. I read it in Willie Thompson's column in the Examiner last year.

"As for my voice, you can blame my daddy, who couldn't distinguish between inside and out, I guess, since he smoked unfiltereds from the time I was born. Right by my crib, Mama said, even though she told him smoking was only for outdoors and in the car with the windows rolled down. I can bring a doctor's note. Something about not getting tubes in my ears when I needed them. Sick from the smoke and whatnot. Allergies. So I can't hear good, and I talk a little off, I know, and a little loud, which I believe would be covered under the Americans with Disabilities Act."

Everett squirmed, just like they do in the movies when a big-time lawyer stares down a rotten cop in a court of law. He took a napkin from the dispenser that was shaped like a NASCAR racecar and wiped his brow.

"Look," he said. "I like you, Gilly, I do. Ever since we were kids back in Mrs. Whitlow's class and you beat up Tommy Hawkins for picking on your little brother. And I don't care what you do with Hoss or whoever else you spend your time with, but you cannot be saying things out loud like"—and here's where he picked up the paper again, and read—"Oh, Hoss, if you were here I'd be losing my religion. I'd be climbing you like a tree."

I looked around. The Stop and Swap was dead silent; all my co-workers were probably in the break room with the door cracked, listening to Everett talk to me like I was a criminal. Soon, the after-school crowd would wander in. Kids forced to eat right in the new and improved lunchroom would be in here raiding the candy shelves, like shaky addicts who got the key to the dealer's stash.

I sat still as a rock, staring Everett down.

"So sign the thing," he finally said, "and we'll forget this ever happened. If you sign it, I can take it to corporate and tell them we had this talk. That's all I need." Everett pushed the paper to my side of the table and handed me a pen. "You're a good employee, all things considered."

Well, Everett didn't know the half of it. Lucy, the eight-to-five lady, stole Snickers bars every single day. Tracy "borrowed" money from petty cash all the time. Hazel snuck off and visited the casino on her lunch break. Half the time she didn't come back. That's what's wrong with America, in my opinion. Hard working people who give a dang and have a opinion about things get run over. And I work hard. That's why the health inspector ain't breathing down our necks. I throw out the hot dogs after three days in the cooker. I dump out the old grease in the deep fryer. I freakin' mop the bathroom floor!

But I did not say any of that. No, I did not. I stood up then, pushed the nachos into the trash as I did. I put my hand on my hip—a Penelope move if ever there was one—and looked down on Everett and felt just a little bit sorry for him. He wasn't a bad guy, just a company guy who didn't know squat about working in the real world.

Everett stood up too. He shoved his hands in his pockets, a move I'd seen a hundred times in school when some yahoo asked him for lunch money. "Give me a quarter," they'd say. "Give me a dime." He always handed it over, which makes you wonder how he ever got into management. He tried to stare me down, but he's not very good at it, so he sat down again and started shuffling papers.

Outside, Hoss had shown up. He was revving the engine on his Harley, just the way I liked it. He had a tattoo of his grandma, looking over her shoulder, tossing scratch to a flock of chickens scattered across on his bicep. She'd been a proud woman, one who probably didn't expect to show up on someone's flesh, shaking her butt every time he gunned the engine.

"I don't know," I said, and reached out for the papers he was holding. "I got a lawyer looks things over for me. And you've

upset me something awful, I got to be honest. And like I
mentioned, I got a disability that I believe the United States
Constitution protects unless the U.S. got invaded by the USSR
and nobody bothered to tell me. So I'm leaving now. I'll be back
tomorrow." Then I chewed my lip a little and changed my mind.
"I might be back, depending on what the lawyer says."

Everett looked confused, like a kid in a corn maze on a
moonless night.

"OK," he said, in a little creak of a voice. "I don't want any
trouble."

And then I grabbed my jean jacket and I walked—no I
sashayed—out the door, the bell ringing behind me, and leaned
against Hoss's bike. When I told him what had happened, he
shook his head. "Damn fool," he said. "Think he could ever find
anybody better than you?" He revved his motor again. "Want me
to go in there and give him what for?"

Something like that will make your heart melt. A man all
riled up, ready to defend your honor. I shook my head no. No
need to get Hoss in trouble with the law again. And then I took
his face in my hands and I kissed him hard, right in front of the
Stop and Swap. A bunch of kids had come over from the high
school, the ones not yet old enough to drive. They started
cheering us on, me in my little red uniform I'd hemmed up a
smidgen too high and Hoss clutching me like I might run away if
he let go.

"Nah," I said. "Everett, he ain't worth the trouble."

And that's when Hoss motioned for me to climb on behind
him, and so I did, the two of us tearing out of there like the last
scene in a picture show that makes you cheer for the underdog,
that makes you proud you live in the great U.S. of A.

Up on Piney Mountain

Allie Walker pushed aside two trashcans that held chicken feed, scooted past the riding lawn mower, and grabbed her ex-husband's handsaw. The shed was dark, even when the sun was out, surrounded as it was by oaks and pines.

She'd always loved the way a saw sounded when you bent it and then let it loose, that twang it made, like music, like Patsy Cline, all sorrowful and strong at the same time.

Inside her house were two dozen people, all dressed in black, filing past the deviled eggs right about now, sipping wine and whiskey sours and talking about God knows what. She hated every one of them, including Deacon Tomm, who'd been drinking while he pontificated, so his rambling sounded like an infomercial for Jesus.

Allie put the saw in the back of her Ford Escape. Her son, Joey, called the SUV the Allie-mobile, ever since she'd decorated it with decals she'd made herself. She'd brought home vinyl scraps that her boss at Jinx Sign Shop called "negative space." These were the odd-shaped pieces that were torn away to reveal letters and pictures. After six years of work, there was hardly a spot on the old car that didn't have an alien or a headless horseman or an angel with flames where its wings should have been.

The road leading to the town square was quiet. It was that murky time of day, and clouds were tumbling in. Trash skittered across the street. An ad for the new pizza place flew across her windshield, and Allie hit the brakes. She looked at her hands. She was gripping the steering wheel so hard her knuckles stuck out.

The magnolia, planted on the day in 1896 when the town was formed, stood at the center of the square like a villain, brooding and invincible. The gash where the pickup had hit it was white and deep. There were fake flowers where the trunk met the ground, and baseballs, and notes written on poster board with glitter paint. *Life is but a dream*, one message read, and Allie felt her stomach clench. "Stupid," Allie said. "Life is anything but a dream." She stepped from the car, grabbed the saw and a long length of rope, and walked to the tree.

It was her birthday. She was thirty-seven. Middle age was so close she could feel it. Her shoulder ached in winter, and her right knee popped when she climbed stairs. Today, though, she felt equal to the magnolia, and she hoisted herself up on the lowest limb. The saw hung from the rope that she'd looped through the opening in the handle, and the thing now swung across her back.

Allie climbed slowly, watching her feet. It wouldn't do to slip. The sky rumbled, and a flash of lightning fell across the eastern sky, too far away to matter. She stood as upright as she could in the big tree, bracing her back against an "L" where a branch grew straight out, slid down to a sitting position, and grabbed the saw.

Allie surveyed the old magnolia. She began sawing just past the place where she sat, the scrape of metal on wood the only sound she wanted to hear.

When the limb finally fell, she leaned back, letting the tree support her. The fallen part of branch hit the ground with a thump, bounced once, lay still. She let out a sigh, looked around. It was getting dark, although it was barely five o'clock on that spring day. Her arm was hurting. She liked the feel of it, the burn that ran from shoulder to wrist. The rain started then, big drops that went splat, the sound loud as knocks at a door you couldn't open. The lightning that had been a mile away only minutes before moved right overhead. Had it not been for the cover of leaves, she would have been soaked, but so far she was only damp.

She held the saw straight out, pushing it through the waxy green leaves. What she wanted at that moment was for the lightning to find her. She could imagine it, the electricity striking the metal, running through her hand, ripping into her heart. If a spark from the saw started a fire, all the better. It could light up this tree, and the tree would flash orange and red and burn to the ground. She said aloud, "I should have brought gasoline."

If your spirit stays where you draw your last breath, then she should have been able to feel Joey here. But she did not feel him, just as she did not feel him in his bedroom, where his jeans still lay crumbled on the rug, and his biology book lay open on his oak desk.

There was speculation, of course, that he'd been drinking when his truck hit the tree. He'd been going sixty in a place where thirty could get you a ticket. He had not been drinking — she had seen the toxicology report. What she feared most was that he'd done it intentionally. That kind of desperation ran through Allie's family, had taken her own father when he was younger than she is now. But Joey was more like his dad: easy going, fearless. His junior college baseball team, the Maysville Tigers, had just won the state championship, a slow pitch game, and he'd been coming home excited, happy, careless.

No, he did not kill himself.

Down below where the rain hit everything, Talbott Benson, the only deputy in town, shined his flashlight and called out. "Allie Walker, is that you up there? I see your car's right here." He paused, rubbed his neck. "You'll catch your death," he said, and then stopped abruptly at the word "death." He shined his flashlight on the ground where the newly cut limb lay. "What the hell do you think you're doing?"

Talbott shook his head. He grabbed the lowest limb. "I'm coming up," he said. A bolt of lightning hit the lightning rod atop the courthouse just across the way. Thunder roared, the earth shook, and Talbott let out a string of cuss words that sounded just about right to Allie.

The deputy was younger than Allie by two years and handsome in a way that made you turn your head when you tried to look at him straight on. Today his face was shadowed by his hat and the gloaming of the late afternoon. Today, nobody was beautiful. When he reached a foothold just below Allie, he said, "I believe you're committing a crime of some kind."

"What if I am?" Allie asked. "You gonna arrest me?"

Talbott blew out his breath, reached into his shirt pocket, pulled out a cigarette, despite the sounding rain. He sat down, straddling one of the middle branches, cupped his hand, and flicked his lighter. He took a long draw, and the smoke seemed to stay in a cloud in front of his face. "I don't believe I am," he said, finally.

Rain pelted Allie, thunder roared farther away this time, and she suddenly felt as heavy as an ox.

"Helluva view when the sun's out," Talbott said, craning his neck to see Allie. "I used to climb this tree all the time. I used to hide from my daddy up here. He was bad to drink, did you know that?"

"The whole town knew that," Allie said. She let go of the handsaw and let it hang limp from its rope. She made a motion like she had a noose at her neck, craned her head to one side. "My daddy did himself in. I don't know why."

"Enough trouble in this world to fill the Grand Canyon," Talbott said, and those words, *the Grand Canyon*, caused Allie's heart to jump. She'd taken Joey there when he was seven. He'd stood on the overlook and spread his arms out and said, "This is bigger than God's cereal bowl!"

When he was eight, he came in from feeding his quarter horse. He took Allie by the hand and led her outside. Queenie stood beneath the morning sun, which was shining so bright the horse seemed to almost disappear into it. Joey said, "Queenie sure is pretty at night, but this morning light defeats her."

Allie had taken to writing down Joey's words. She had a gallon jar on her dresser, hundreds of slips of paper with his observations, his sweet, sweet words that seemed like something a prophet might say.

She had cried so much in the last three days, trying to do it now was like having the dry heaves. Her face ached, her nose felt like it did when she plunged into the city pool and drew in a wave of chlorine.

"I can't stand this world," she said.

"I don't blame you," Talbott said, "nobody blames you," and then he dropped his cigarette and reached up and touched Allie's leg. Allie closed her eyes. "Let's get down from here," Talbott said.

He made it to the ground first, and he held his arms up in case she fell. She swung down easily, but slipped on the wet grass, and lay there, the rain hitting her hard. Talbott scrambled to get her up, took her by the hand, finally, and led her to the police car just as a new wave of lightning hit. He jumped, but she didn't. There was a thermos in the front seat, and she wrapped her hands around it for warmth. He turned on the motor, cranked up the heat. He turned the scanner and radio off.

"Take me somewhere," Allie said, "away from this," and she pointed at the tree.

"Don't you think you ought to go home?"

"I don't ever want to go home again."

At Lotto-Food & More, Talbott went in and picked up a bag of pretzels, a bottle of whiskey, and roll of paper towels so Allie could dry off.

"Take a sip," he said when he got back in the car.

Allie uncapped the bottle, drank, shivered.

"I could get fired for this," he said, and pointed at Allie, at the bottle, at the turned-off equipment.

"You want a drink?"

"Don't touch the stuff," Talbott said. "My daddy and all."

They drove then, out past the city limits, on the back roads they both knew so well.

"You may be crazy right now, Allie," Talbott said. "That's understandable." Allie took another sip of whiskey and considered this.

"I may be crazy from now on," she said, and then she grew quiet. The road bumped beneath them; it was a patchwork of potholes and crumbling asphalt. After a while, she said, "Tell me about the last time you were happy."

Talbott grabbed a paper towel from the roll and wiped the back of his neck. "I got this cabin up on Piney Mountain. Not very big, half a century old. The walls are cedar inside and out. The floors are black oak. I go there on my days off. There's this deer that's taken to me, a doe. She'll eat out of my hand. Last week I went for a walk up the ridge. Well, this doe comes with me, like a dog would, and she keeps nudging me from behind, and when I sit down on this big mossy rock, she keeps rubbing her head against my shirt. And I thought, I haven't seen a lot of evidence of God in my life, but maybe this is enough. This ridge, this doe, the sky blue as a lady's dress."

"The doe could die," Allie said. She looked out the window. "Come hunting season."

"I haven't worked that part out yet."

"My family has a history of doing themselves in," Allie said. "Not just my daddy. My aunt Ida. A cousin in California."

"And my daddy drank," Talbott said, "but I do not."

Allie's hair was beginning to dry. It fell past her shoulders, straight, brown, shiny. Her jeans were just barely damp, but her socks had gotten wet, and she'd taken them off. "It's my birthday," she said. "Thirty-seven, but today I feel a hundred."

"Thirty-five in April," Talbott said.

"Joey won't ever be thirty-five," Allie said, and then coughed, and then took another sip of whiskey.

"I'm more than sorry," Talbott said. "Wish there was

something I could do."

"Nothing anybody can do."

"I got a friend, an old guy I met on a fishing trip to Canada, who's from the Dakota tribe," Talbott said. "He believes the spirit world is only three feet above us, and that's where the dead go, and they become our guardian angels. They have a ritual that lasts for four days, making sure the spirit is settled in good and proper. Everybody feels better when it's over."

"What do you think?" Allie asked.

"I think that sometimes horrible things happen to the best people on earth," Talbott said. "I don't know why. I don't know how we're supposed to get through it, but I do know we have to help the ones left behind. We can't leave a crazy woman up in a tree, for example," and attempted to laugh.

The whiskey had settled Allie down. She lay her head back against the seat and listened to the windshield wipers whoosh. "I wouldn't mind Joey being three feet above me. You were below me in that devil tree, and I could hear every word you said."

"Joey was a good kid," Talbott said.

"It hurts to hear his name. It hurts not to hear his name. I'll have to move. I can't face that tree every day."

"I've been told you can't make big decisions for at least a year after something like this happens," Talbott said.

"Well, tomorrow, I may decide not to get up."

Talbott ignored the meaning of that sentence. "Stay in bed as long as you want," he said. "Get some rest. When you wake up, do it slow. Make sure you eat something every day. Soup is good. Hot tea is good."

When he turned the squad car around, Allie protested. "Don't take me home," she said, and so he veered off the highway, cut across the valley, and started up the slick mountain road.

Allie took another drink just as the road turned to gravel, and another when the gravel turned to mud. When they got to the cabin, Talbott came to her side of the car and opened the door. He took her hiking boots and put them on her feet. The rain was steady, but the storm had passed. When she tried to stand, she couldn't do it, so he lifted her easily and carried her across the porch and into the cedar cabin.

She hadn't been lifted up since she was a kid, back before her father died. She used to pretend she'd fallen asleep on long car rides, just to feel his strong hands lifting her from the backseat, just to feel safe in his big arms.

The thought of it made her stubborn tears start, and Talbott stroked her hair while she cried. He set her down on the couch and made tea. The rain was serious now, and the wind howled.

She slept, eventually, and when she woke, Talbott was still there, out cold in the old recliner that listed to one side.

Allie went out on the porch. The rain had stopped, and the air was cold and pure. She found a tree stump Talbott used as a side table, cleared away the ashtray, and stood atop it. Allie held her hand straight up. She knew she was at least three feet taller that way and imagined Joey in the mist of morning, in a place where everything made sense and nobody died. As long as she stood like that, she felt a warm hand wrapped around hers. The feeling might have been grief, she understood that. But it might have come from the clarity grief brings.

As soon as the thought materialized, Talbott's doe showed up, buff-colored and glorious. She climbed the steps to stand beside Allie. Talbott rose from his chair as this was happening. Allie was not on the couch. He checked his gun; it was still in its holster.

He said aloud, "Thank God."

When he bounded onto the porch, he saw Allie standing still, her hand raised, her hair tangled. The doe did not even turn to greet him, just stood transfixed, watching. Allie stood like that for longer than seemed humanly possible, in the soft light of morning, and Talbott bore witness to it all, though he would never speak of it again, not to anyone in this broken old world but Allie.

Carry Me Over

"Let the dead bury the dead," J.T. says, and then honks and tries to switch lanes. We are inching across the Midland Boulevard bridge that crosses the Arkansas River. This used to be the easy way to get from Fort Smith to Van Buren, but then the road crew started fixing up Interstate 40, shutting down lanes, and now this road is packed like rush hour in New York City pretty much all the time.

"What?" I ask.

J.T. says again, "Let the dead bury the dead. That's scripture, ain't it?"

"Matthew 8:22."

"Right," J.T. answers, and then he cranks up his Hank Williams CD.

"I miss Hank," I say.

"You miss everybody," J.T. says.

The tail pipe on the termite truck just ahead of us is blowing smoke. "What do you mean by that?"

"Everybody you love is dead."

"That isn't so."

J.T. nods his head toward the truck bed. In it five wreaths lay, ready for the cemetery.

Just then, somewhere way back behind us, brakes squeal, metal hits metal, and the bridge, already quivering from the weight of us all, shimmies a little more.

"Another fender bender," J.T. says. "I wish I was in the body repair business."

My daddy used to cross the Arkansas River, drive straight over it when it froze solid in the dead of winter. It doesn't freeze anymore, not even when we hit zero.

One of the wreaths is for him, God rest his weary soul.

The light at the end of the bridge has gone green, and we are moving now. The Crawford County Courthouse appears, the church with stained glass windows nearby, just big pieces of glass in bright colors. If a kid was to draw a church, it would look like this one.

"I work a full week for what you spend on graveyard flowers," J.T. says. He's not from here. He's not from anywhere. A drifter. His daddy was a sharecropper. Moved the family across the South. Moved them twice in one year when J.T. was sixteen. He's been here with me longer than he's been anywhere. His people get burned to ashes, get tossed into oceans, get set on fireplace mantles in little vases when they die. Cemeteries, they don't mean much to a man like him.

We pass La Huerta, a Mexican restaurant J.T. pronounces La Hurt Ya. "Could've ate there if we hadn't bought them flowers," he says.

"We have to buy the flowers," I say, and J.T. snorts.

"Sure we do," he says. "Sure."

I used to see some sparkle in J.T. I used to sparkle myself when he'd come calling. We'd stay up nights, and I'd tell him stories. I'd tell him how my grandma was once walking down Garrison Avenue in Fort Smith, how the elastic popped on her underpants, and how when they dropped to her ankles, she stepped out of them, just kept walking, and acted like nothing happened. The purple wreath is for her. That woman loved purple.

At Paul's Bakery we go in and get two cream horns and two bottled Cokes, and I say hi to the two Bettys behind the counter. There used to be a mural painted on the front of the building. Deer in deep woods, a squirrel up a tree, a hunting dog down below, that's how I remember it. A man named Bye Golly painted it. My grandpa said he had the hands of God and a taste for whiskey. I don't know if that's true.

One of the wreaths is for Grandpa. The one shaped like an artist's pallet is for Bye Golly.

We pass by First Baptist, a big blond brick building that takes up a full city block. I fell down laughing inside the sanctuary when I was eight. My friend Calvin was getting baptized. I'd never seen anybody dunked before and I broke up as he went under. I got a whipping for it later.

One of the wreaths is for Calvin, who made it through the baptismal waters but not Vietnam.

"Why you go to the graveyard so much?" J.T. asks.

"Decoration Day's next week," I say. "I like to go early. I like being first at something. I tell you that every year."

"I been thinking we should get out of here, try living somewhere else. Like Tennessee," J.T. says. "Never lived in Tennessee. And there's a guy there has a raccoon named Gun

Show, has another raccoon named Rebekah who takes showers with him and drinks Pepsi Cola."

"You do aspire to greatness," I say, my voice a little hateful, even to my ears.

"We could make friends," J.T. says. "We could raise goats. You always liked goats. You could quit your stinking job down at the auction house."

"But," I say, and J.T. asks, "But what?"

And that is where I stop. We are pulling into Gracelawn Cemetery, easing through the entrance where Arkansas limestone makes up the two giant pillars. Up ahead is Grandma's plot. Her stone has that verse on it that begins, "Two ships that pass in the night." She went through three husbands in the fifty-five years she spent on this earth. She's buried beside the second one. Grandma picked out her own stone, back when she was still working at Moore's Café six days a week. "I want something substantial," she said. "Something that says I lived a life reading books instead of pouring coffee for truck drivers with wandering hands."

Her best friend Inez is buried beside her. Inez never married. The fifth wreath is for her. Her stone is pink marble. She lived eighteen years after my grandma died. The back of her stone says only this: Gone to Wal-Mart.

We step out, and I wait for J.T. to hand me the first wreath. He's got his pliers, and he's cut a section of a wire clothes hanger that he's bending into a 'U' shape so he can secure the wreath to the ground.

He kneels and hooks the wire through the purple bow. J.T. will leave for Tennessee one day soon, I know he will. He'll probably buy an old trailer and learn to love raccoons. The thought makes me catch my breath, makes my heart hurt.

I asked him once where he'd scattered his mother's ashes, and he said he'd driven her across Arizona, a place she'd never been but wanted to go, sifting her out a little at a time. "When there wasn't but a few tablespoons left of her, I took her to Oak Creek Canyon and let her go," he said, "every bit of dust gone. The campers next to me come over to watch. I sang 'I'll Fly Away.' The littlest kid, he was maybe four, pulled a few yellow weeds and threw them into the creek." He shook his head. "The grave swallows you up. The water carries you over. I ain't one for getting swallowed up."

We walk to Calvin's grave. I wish I could go back and watch his blond head dipped in the water again and understand the gravity of it all. I wrote him every day he was in Vietnam. The last three letters I wrote were never opened.

J.T. is a ropey man, long-limbed, weathered face. Here in the cemetery, he looks older than he usually does. When it gets cold, he limps a little. An old bull riding injury, he says, but who knows for sure. He reaches over, takes the wreath from my hand and tacks it to the ground.

"Not everyone I love is dead," I say, and I rub J.T.'s back.

"That so?"

"It is," I say.

"You got something to tell me, girl?" he asks, and he smiles then, for the first time in a long time.

I love this time of day, the sun dipping low. I have lived my whole life here. When I first gave J.T. directions to my house, I said, "Turn right just past where Bo Monte's Restaurant used to be." He laughed at me and said, "How the hell would I know where anything in this town used to be?"

"I do have something to tell you," I say. "I will not house a raccoon, nor will I bathe with one."

"That sounds reasonable," he says, and then he scuffs the grass with his work boot. "But you will go," he says, the sentence right on the verge of being a question.

One of the caretakers drives up in his rusty truck. He waves at me and rolls down his window. "How are you, Miss Mary?" he asks. I recognize him. He's one of the Odom boys, though I can't place which one.

"Never better," I say. "Going to be moving soon. To Tennessee, up in the hills."

"Do tell," he says.

"Sure am," I say.

"Well, good for you," he says, and then I think he notices I'm crying.

"I'll look after the plots for you," he says. "Make sure the stones don't sink. Clean 'em up with that organic spray, keeps the moss away, don't hurt a thing. I'll even set out your flowers if you need me to. Or we could plant some rose bushes along here," he says, and points to the row of stones.

"I do appreciate it," I say.

"I've been to Tennessee," the Odom boy says, "up where Dolly has the theme park. Nice, nice place."

And then J.T. says, "We're going to raise goats. We're going to do all kinds of things."

The Odom boy tips his cap and drives away. He will go home and tell his mama, and she'll tell her sister, and by morning time the whole town will know.

J.T. takes me by the shoulders. He pulls me to him and holds me tight against his chest. I think I might fall to the ground if he takes his hands away. But he does not. He stands still as a rock, and he holds me steady while the day disappears.

I thought about how I'd wake tomorrow, a woman changing her circumstances. "Let the dead bury the dead," I say into J.T.'s shirt collar, but if he hears me, he doesn't say a word. He doesn't say anything at all in this land of my people, on the altar of everything I ever was.

When the Lights Go On Again All Over the World

We are lying belly down on the fishing dock at Cedar Lake, our arms hanging over the edge, the tip ends of our fingers rippling the water. I'm wearing a red bikini even though it's barely April, and my hair is up in a messy bun I worked on for an hour, not that Otis seems to notice. He'd been watching a TV show about a Canadian woman who got engaged ten times during World War II before he called me and asked me to spend the day with him. Every soldier the Canadian promised to marry died in the war. Otis says, "That woman was steeped in hope."

"That woman was a harbinger of death," I say, and Otis hits the water with the heel of his hand. "She surely was not. If you'd of watched the show, you'd know that."

"I don't see how ten boys dying has one lick of hope in it."

Otis rolls onto his back, pushes the air out of his lungs, and then puts his big ole hands beneath his head. I sit up beside him. I can smell the lake water below us, and on my hands, and in the air around us. Otis says, "Think what those last days would have been like if they hadn't had the Canadian woman's letters."

"You never once wrote me a letter, and we've been going out for nearly a year."

"Nola," Otis says, "what would I say that I can't tell you straight on?"

I squint my eyes like I do when I don't want to see the world the way it is. The edges of everything go hazy, and then I say, "You amaze me, Otis, you really do, but not in a good way."

Cedar Lake is in a valley that catches every bit of cool air and holds it captive. Up on the ridge where I live, it's scalding already. Otis brought a cooler with him, and inside are a dozen Pabst Blue Ribbon beers. I take one out, pop the top, take a swig.

"I don't know why we argue," Otis says.

The boards on the dock are old and worn smooth and feel like cotton sheets straight from the clothesline. I set the beer down and lie on my back beside him. "Maybe we don't like each other very much."

Otis pulls me on top of him. "I like you just fine," he says, and then he takes off my sunglasses and kisses me. Kissing, and every bit of what follows, is another way to make the rough edges of the world disappear. After a while, Otis and me seem to be part of something eternal, as tied to the earth as the water below us and the sky above.

On the way out, I sit beside Otis in his old Ford truck, so close our thighs touch. I'm thirty-five now, and I've been sidled up like this to one guy or another for nearly half my life.

The pickup windows are down, and the air in the valley smells like sour apple gum. I've driven as far away as Abilene, and I've never found this smell anywhere else. I lay my head on Otis's shoulder, and he wraps his arm around me.

Otis starts talking, still stuck on topic of that dang woman from the TV show. "When the Canadian lady wrote to her soldiers, she always started the letters with 'My Dearest Someone.'" Otis has the words "heat lightning" tattooed on his arm, the block letters following the bone from elbow to wrist. There was a local band named Heat Lightning he used to love, and one night he got knee-walking drunk and went over to Ziggy's Ink Palace. Well, Heat Lightning hasn't played in more than ten years. The lead singer preaches now at one of those churches without a denomination tied to it. It's called Streets of Gold, or Highway to Heaven. Something like that.

"Those were different times," I say, talking about World War II.

"Every one of the guys asked for her picture. They trimmed the photos down and carried them in their cigarette cases. They carried those boxes in the pocket closest to their hearts."

"Was she beautiful?"

"She looked a lot like my Aunt Edna used to. Dark wavy hair. Green eyes a little too close together. But she had this smile that seemed like it made the whole world spin."

We stop at Sonic and get a couple of corndogs and a tub of tater tots. I drink another beer, the can icy in my hand. We're in a dry county in the middle of the afternoon, but what the hell. The carhop gives me a look, and I tip the bottle at her, like a salute. "Give her an extra dollar," I say to Otis, and he does it and then laughs.

Otis eats the tater tots two at a time. "Most of the letters were sweet," he says. "The soldiers told her she was swell, or that they'd gotten a radio and were listening to Bob Hope but thinking about her. But then, later, as they got closer to the end, they'd tell her things that would gut-punch you. This one sergeant told her he dwelled in a world of death, and then he went on to describe it." Otis shudders. "He said he didn't know how he'd live anymore with regular humanity, seeing what he'd seen, doing what he'd done, even if he did make it home.

"She wrote him back, and she told him that he would come home. She said she sat on her porch every evening, and she looked at the moon. She swore she could see the future in it. She said, 'And there we are, around the kitchen table. You've gained twenty pounds since you came home. There's a highchair beside you with the cutest little bitty baby sitting in it. Looks just like you. Outside, the mailman is walking down the street, and he's whistling because he doesn't have one letter in his bag with bad news in it. And on the radio, Vera Lynn is singing "When the Lights Go on Again (All Over the World)."'"

Otis drips a packet of mustard on his corndog. "My granddaddy was in that war. My granddaddy near about raised me, what with Daddy taking off over the years, going to and fro, who knows where. If Granddaddy would've got killed, I wouldn't be here. I wouldn't of known Granddaddy, the best man I ever met."

I take another swig, the beer cold as I swallow. This may be the saddest date I've ever been on. I give up and quit holding in my stomach. I reach behind the seat where I put my bag, and I pull on my T-shirt from Carrie Underwood's last concert tour, covering my bikini.

"My grandpa was in World War II," I say, and suddenly I can see the photos of him. He weighed one hundred and two pounds when he enlisted. He was seventeen. He ended up in Okinawa. I don't know what he was like before, but life after was its own battleground.

"The world today," Otis says, and then he stops. He dumps the

65

corndog in the Sonic sack and takes my unfinished beer and chugs it down.

I look out the window at the advertisements that are up everywhere. Sonic is having a half-price shake special every night after eight. A shake sounds good, like all that ice cream might fill the cavern that just opened up inside me. "Mama says she remembers when ISIS was just a kids' cartoon about an Egyptian superhero. She'd watch her on Saturday mornings, a beautiful woman in a costume, doing what she could to save humanity."

"I remember when you could go to the movies without fearing a gunman might come in behind you."

"Why do you think the Canadian kept promising her future to the doomed?"

Otis taps his fingers on the driver's doorframe. "World War II was everybody's war. I think she was fighting it the best way she knew how."

"Did she ever marry?"

Otis shakes his head no. "She ran a daycare. And wrote letters to the editor of the newspaper, asking people to be kind to one another."

The world is at a tipping point. Both me and Otis know it. We watch the news together when I spend the night, the overly tan newswoman grim as she waits for the video to roll. In the last weeks, we've seen death come in waves, here at home and as far away as Turkey, and we've not even left Otis's living room.

I pat his knee. "I get it now."

"What?"

"The Canadian."

"Good," Otis says and touches my cheek.

"What can we do about this sorry old world?" I ask, and Otis seems to know exactly what I mean.

"I'll show you."

There's a couple, pushing seventy, sitting at the picnic table where walk-ups eat, sharing a kid's meal. They look like trouble's ridden on their backs for years. They have a dog with them, the kind of mutt you see in every shelter ad that's ever been made. The dog, the man, the woman, look worn out. The woman slips the dog a french fry and rubs its lopsided head.

Otis motions the carhop over. The girl has black hair and black nail polish and black eyeliner that rings her dark eyes. He pulls out the hundred-dollar bill he keeps hidden behind his fishing license in his wallet, and he hands it over. It's his emergency money. His safety net. He points. "Give this to that couple there," he says, "just don't say who it come from."

The girl looks at the couple and then turns back and looks at us. "Why?" she asks. And Otis says, "We're passing out hope today."

"You meet all kinds," the carhop says.

We watch as the girl takes the money to the table, holds it out like a flag. The couple looks suspicious, and then they lean in, asking questions, I'm sure, but the carhop just shrugs her shoulders. When the man takes the hundred-dollar bill, he kisses it, and then puts it in his pocket. The dog gets up, struggling on shaky legs, and starts to circle the trio, its sorry tail wagging.

Otis starts the engine. The motor races and then settles down. Otis reaches for the gearshift but stops. He takes my hand in his, and we sit, cradled in this valley of hope. Outside, on the fringes of this spot, sorrow waits, and trouble so big it can bust you apart. We all know it's there, but that doesn't mean we shouldn't try to stop it.

Early Morning in the Land of Dreams

The building where I work is an old Walmart. The new Super Walmart is only two and a half miles away, right off the interstate, up by the church that has its own helicopter, up near the strip mall with a shop where you can get sixteen kinds of pasta flown in from Italy, or Tulsa, who knows for sure.

My boss told me to quit calling the building "the old Walmart." "Gypsy," she said, "it's Dream Catchers, or D.C. if Dream Catchers is too much of a burden for you to say."

And then she goes through the whole protocol again. She sits next to me, she picks up my phone and pretends there's a caller on the other end. "Dream Catchers," she says, her voice happy like she's just won something. And then she adds the company slogan, "Where your dreams are our business."

I roll my eyes.

"Is that so hard?" she asks.

"No ma'am," I say, and flash a smile that I hope looks genuine.

My cubicle is where the Maybelline aisle used to be. Right next to what used to be the pharmacy. Six aisles over from the auto center, three aisles from the light bulbs. If I took a pencil out, I could draw you the whole store, the way it used to be. It was about the biggest place to go in this town when I was growing up, so I know it like I know my own name. Even came here the night of my senior prom, hair done up, sequined dress, heels that would kill me if I tried to walk in them now. I bought a packet of breath mints and added a candy bar in case my date didn't offer to buy me dinner.

My job is to take calls from people who need somebody to hear what it felt like to wake from a dream where you were twenty again, or where you had a job slaughtering hogs, or where you fell from a pecan tree and landed on your first boyfriend.

The owner of Dream Catchers, a trust fund baby from Georgia, had a bunch of geniuses work with a team of brain experts to create an algorithm that takes certain words—like "blindfold" or "jet" or "ice cream"—to see what the masses want, what they fear, what they long for. "This will be bigger than Einstein's Theory of Relativity," he said at the ribbon cutting the day we opened, and the mayor of our little town got so excited he near about cried. They showed the mayor over and over on the local news, his eyes misty, his hand going straight to his eyes, and then finally his hand to his heart, like someone in love.

Nobody knows for sure what the owner will do with the information we're gathering, though there's speculation he might use it to sway elections or sell deodorant. I don't really care as long as I get my paycheck on time.

Before these callers can share their night visions, they have to answer a bunch of questions they lie about. Last week, this old guy who said he was fifty but sounded at least ninety, swore he jogged six days a week. When I asked him what kind of running shoes he wore, he said, "Keds, just like everybody else in my running club."

I charted it all for Mr. Senior Citizen, calculating his food intake, water intake, how many medications he took, what he ate before bed. "A Coca-Cola and a handful of peanuts," he said.

Forty-seven percent of my callers drink some kind of soda pop before bed. Only two percent eat peanuts. Sixty-four percent sleep alone. These are facts I carry with me, telling people at parties, telling the doctor who gives me Xanax when my own dreams get too bad.

At work, the same woman keeps calling every morning at 3:33. She's having man trouble, not dream trouble, though she tries to throw me off by adding one strange detail to each of her stories to make them sound a little more believable. I don't make her go through the questionnaire anymore, something that could get me suspended if my boss listens in on my calls, which I'm pretty sure she does.

"I had a dream," Mrs. 3:33 says to me tonight, "that my husband found the credit card bill and I had a charge of $159.87 to a place in Kentucky that sells medical-grade vitamins, which are supposed to reverse the aging process. They're also supposed to make you happier, and who doesn't want to be happy?" she asks but doesn't wait for an answer.

"He called me an ugly name, my husband did," she says, "a seriously ugly name that I have never been called in my entire life, not even when I was a cocktail waitress back in the 1970s, which should give you some idea just how awful it was."

She stalls for just a second and then says, "And over in the corner was Sandra Bullock, the dark-haired Sandra Bullock, not the blonde one.

"Anyway, I said to my husband, 'Joe Joe McPherson, you spent way more money than that painting the den black and buying a giant TV than I ever in my life spent on vitamins.'

"I was talking about our new theater room," she says to me. "Well, he swelled up like he does, and then he said the strangest thing. He said, 'That just kicks the can a little farther down the road, now doesn't it?' Next thing I know, he's out the bedroom door, and then I hear the garage door whine open and then shut back. I felt my heart drop, I swear I did, when I realized he was leaving again."

Mrs. 3:33 says she's forty-one, which means she's in her fifties. She belongs to a gym but hesitates when I ask her how often she goes, which means she doesn't go at all. She cooks everything she can in a cast iron skillet. Her grandma told her once that it was the key to a long life, and she's believed it ever since.

"What did he mean?" she asks. "That just kicks the can a little farther down the road?"

"Ma'am," I say, "I'm not allowed to interpret dreams."

My boss walks by and gives me a thumbs-up. It's rare praise, and so I return the gesture. When she moves on, I say, "But I will tell you this. I had a man used to tear me down like I was a tarpaper shack in the path of a twister. I married him on the rebound, something I would never, ever recommend. But I did it, six months after my first husband—his name was Ernest—left.

"That was the saddest I've ever been in my life, so broke down I didn't even feel like myself. I passed by a mirror one day at work, and I thought I was looking at someone else. I was hunched over like an old woman, the corners of my mouth hung down. My clothes swallowed me, I'd gotten so skinny. Overnight, and I swear to God this is the truth, a whole patch of gray showed up in my hair. Just like that.

"One night I pulled myself up, put on my face and went to the midnight movie. And that's where, just as the Titanic sank, I realized I wasn't as downtrodden as I'd thought. When I got home, I slept in the spare room. Well, he didn't like it one little bit. But you know what? By then, I didn't care what he thought. In a year we were done, done, done."

My caller is silent. The fluorescent light above me buzzes. Outside, in the parking lot, I can hear a car whoosh by. The kids around here, they like this parking lot. It's almost empty, most of the big lights that used to keep it bright as daylight have burned out. So they show up at odd hours, they drive like NASCAR drivers, they whip around this big building like they're never going to die.

Finally, Mrs. 3:33 says, "The vitamins aren't helping at all."

"How old are you?" I ask, and this time she tells the truth.

"Fifty-four," she says.

"You work?"

"I sell undergarments at Cleo's, the downtown Cleo's, but just on weekends. Been doing it for twenty-three years."

"I may have bought a girdle from you," I say.

"Foundation garment," she says, and then laughs. "We're not allowed to say girdle. Company rule."

"Well, I say a lot of things I'm not supposed to. Sometimes you've got to buck the system. You should try it sometime."

Mrs. 3:33 says, "I don't think I'm as brave as you."

"You're probably just smarter," I say, and then I add, "Let me tell you one last thing, life's too short to wear foundation garments, and it's damn straight too short to tolerate a man you don't love."

There is silence for what seems like a whole minute. And then she says, "But I do love him," and then her voice goes all quivery. "I'm just wondering if he still loves me."

I hesitate. This side of the building is almost empty. Just me, my boss, three people in data entry. None of us is married. Above her desk, my boss has a painting of Cozumel, fat pink flowers shining against a night sky. Here's the thing, though. I know she's never been. The three guys in data entry buy a lottery ticket together every Wednesday, hoping for the big break that will take them out of here. On their desks are baseballs and footballs from games they played in high school, and old birthday cards from the Dream Catchers' headquarters in Atlanta.

"I know where he goes when he leaves at night," she says, and I wait.

"He sits in front of his first wife's house."

"Oh," I say.

"She's dead," she says. "Six months ago. Car wreck. Joe Joe got a call in the middle of the night. He cried. I never heard him cry before. Not one time."

There is more silence, and then she says, "She was younger than me."

I want to tell her about my first husband, Ernest. I want to tell her how he used to talk to me late at night. I had the same bad dreams then as I have now. My childhood, it wasn't so good. I thought if I started talking about it, I might never stop. So I never did.

On those nights, Ernest would sit up with me. He'd tell me

stories from his own childhood that always had a mutt dog named Bug in them, and a mama waiting at home who used to say to him every single night, "I love you so much I could sop you up with a biscuit."

I think about telling Mrs. 3:33 the story, but if I did, I'd have to explain why Ernest left. That story is so full of my own regret and recklessness I'd never tell it to anyone.

Instead, I ask, "How old did you say your husband was?"

"Sixty," she says.

"He retired?"

"No," she says, and then she sighs. There is a TV playing in the background, and through the phone I can hear canned laughter, the kind that gets added to shows that fall flat without it.

"We refinanced the house a few years back," she says. "We took a trip to Barcelona. Bought a Hummer. We added a garage we didn't really need. And then I had some work done. Not too much, though. A little snip-snip to tighten my jawline. I had my teeth capped. He may never get to retire."

My other line is blinking.

"You might want to ease up on the credit card," I say, and she sighs.

"Eternal youth," she says. "What a scam."

I pick up the other line. "Dream Catchers," I say.

In my wallet is an old picture of me and Ernest, from the last time we were happy. In it, we're jumping off the Frogtown bridge together. I have on a blue bikini and my hands are thrown up, and my ribs show, and my hair is a black waterfall fanning out behind me. Ernest, blond and fair as daylight, has his hand on my back, and his eyes are squeezed shut.

There is so much in that picture I love. Me in that tiny bikini, sure, but more than that, stuff you don't see. We had a picnic right before we climbed on the bridge. I'd made tuna fish salad and strawberry pie. And after that, we lay on an old quilt I'd brought along, and we talked about this house we'd seen over in Charleston. Wide porch, big windows, flower boxes. Painted yellow as the sun. Ernest circled my wrist with his fingers, then he said, "We'll have a house like that someday." And right then, it sounded like the easiest thing in the world.

Last I heard Ernest was living somewhere in Texas. Never remarried, far as I know.

I like to think I had something to do with that. I like to think that he couldn't find anybody as exciting as me, that he couldn't love anybody as much as he loved me. But maybe it was the other way around. I could make him crazy sometimes. I could make myself crazy. Maybe I made marriage seem so bad he couldn't bear to try it again.

I wonder what it would be like to sit outside his house. To sit out front in my old car, headscarf on, sunglasses on, just watching. I wonder what it would be like to see him through his windows. Watch him drink orange juice in the morning, watch him come in from work at night. If he saw me in the light of day would he even speak to me? Could I say, sorry, sorry, sorry, until he finally believed me?

Sometimes I think he could.

My boss walks back by while I'm thinking these deep thoughts. She wears slippers with her suits, which chips away at her authority if you ask me. I give her another thumbs-up, but this time she ignores me. This new caller's talking to me now, jumping right in, telling me about his dream about a whippoorwill with four legs, a goat sitting at his kitchen table, a hatchet hanging from his ceiling fan. "There was a crow, too," he says, "and it was wearing a ladies housecoat. But it just hung on him, because he didn't have arms, you see."

I listen, but I don't say anything. These talkers, they can go on for a while.

"This Dream Catchers place," he finally asks, "is that anywhere near the Dream Oasis in Memphis?"

"Nah," I say, "we're in an old Walmart building in a little backwater town in Arkansas. Right behind the McDonald's that stays open all twenty-four hours, although I've never seen one car pull through after midnight."

My boss's back is to me. I see her throw up her hands and shake her head. I think she might turn around, that she might write me up this time, but she keeps walking.

At 4:00, she'll be back in her office. She watches old movies in there, stuff with subtitles. In her desk drawer, she keeps protein bars and Hershey's Kisses. Her chair is a giant exercise ball she perches atop, always trying to find her balance.

When the call is over, I log on to the Internet, another big no-no at Dream Catchers. I type in Ernest's name and then Texas. For only $9.99 I can find out where he lives, if he's ever gone bankrupt, if he's ever been convicted of a crime. It feels like I'm doing something illegal, although I can't say why. My hands shake. I try to swallow, but my mouth's gone dry, and I reach for my bottle of water. When I've recovered, I pull my credit card from my wallet and start typing in the numbers.

And then the phone rings. I hesitate and then tap the "answer" button on my headset. On the line is someone whose dream is the one thing they can't escape tonight. And I'm the only person around to listen to it. I rub my temples. I take a deep breath. And then I kick into gear. "Dream Catchers," I say, in a voice that sounds too weak to be mine. So I start again. "Dream Catchers," I repeat, "where your dreams are our business."

Remnants of Another Time

Glen Campbell showed up at the foot of my bed three nights after he died. He said, real gentle like, "Mary Alice, you're from Phoenix, aren't you?"

I sat up, a shockwave running through me. I blinked twice, thinking Glen might disappear, but he didn't. I was from Phoenix, though I wondered how he knew. I'd moved to Arkansas when I was six, and now I was nearing sixty, a fact I held like a cup of scalding coffee that was bound to burn me sooner or later.

"I wrote a song about Phoenix once," he said, grinning, and just like that, a guitar appeared in his hands.

I held a finger to my lips and nodded toward my husband, Carl, who was wearing his CPAP mask. That mask has ruined our love life more than his snoring ever did.

Glen wore a chestnut-colored leather jacket I remembered from an album cover in the 1970s. His pants were tan polyester, his shirt red, flowered, and unbuttoned to the middle of his farm-boy chest. Death had made him young again. He frowned. "You don't want me to play?" he asked, and I said, "Not if it wakes up Carl."

"We should go outside then," Glen said.

My pajamas were gray and stretched out, and there was writing on the top that read, Help Me Make It Through the Night. It was a line from an old song I used to slow dance to. Now, the words were more like a prayer.

"I don't think I should be hanging out with a man, dead or otherwise, in the middle of the night," I said. "No offense," I added, and Glen said, "Might make for a good story someday. I know how you love stories."

So, I crawled out of bed. We walked through the house until we reached the back door, and then we stepped into the bloom of that August night.

Glen took a breath. "No place in the world like Arkansas."

I have a gardenia that lives only because I set it right by the porch there, where the runoff from the AC drips and drips. It had flowered last Sunday when Glen's address was still on this side of Glory. On the fencerow a few feet away, my antique roses bloomed, all pink, all with French names I couldn't pronounce if you held a .44 to my head.

Glen leaned against the porch railing and breathed. "The perfume of night," he said. "The drifting smell of hay and creek water. Dirt roads after a summer rain. County fairs where everything's fried. Churches that smell like old books and lemon furniture polish. I love them all."

"That right there," I said. "What you just said, all that beauty, that's how come your songs grabbed at people's hearts."

His guitar was slung across his back. "I had a way of looking at the world sideways, I guess. I think it was because I almost drowned once. My brother Lyndell saved me when I was a little kid. After that, my life seemed like a miracle, like a divine gift."

There are two rocking chairs on my porch, painted yellow, the color chipping the way all those home decorators love nowadays. I sat down, and Glen adjusted his guitar and sat next to me. "I saw you once at the Arkansas-Oklahoma State Fair," I said. "They'd turned the lights low, and you rode to the middle of the arena on a white horse. The glitter on your outfit caught the moonlight, caught the lamplight, threw sparkles that looked like shooting stars. My lord, how you could sing."

Glen picked up his guitar and started singing his song about the stark lonely lives of housewives that kills me every time.

The moon was leaning toward red, so pretty the weather guy showed a picture of it on the news the next day. When he finished singing, he said, "If I'd stayed in Arkansas, I might have married a girl like you. Had a bunch of kids. Maybe some cattle."

I smoothed my hair with the back of my hand, felt the heat rise to my face. The tree frogs were so loud they sounded like an engine come to life. "Still a smooth-talker," I said, and he said, "I get that a lot."

The next thing he said was, "Let's walk." I had a decision to make then. I hesitated, but then Glen grinned, and that sealed the deal. I stepped inside for a minute, snuck into the bedroom, and slipped on my tennis shoes. When I came outside, Glen was in the backyard, the stars above him. He looked like a god.

We walked down the dirt road in front of my house. When we reached the crossroads, I led him down another dirt path that took us to Paddock Lake, hidden behind pines and oak. The surface of the water was a mirror for the moonlight, and a family of raccoons huddled on the bank. We eased around them. At the fishing dock, we sat. Glen took off his cowboy boots and socks, rolled up his pants, and put his feet in the water.

"My deepest memories are in Arkansas," he said. "Sitting next to my mama in church on Sunday morning when I was a boy, knowing there'd be dinner on the ground after. Playing that first five-dollar guitar Daddy bought me from Sears and Roebuck."

He moved his feet back and forth, two metronomes keeping time, the dark water swishing. "Once I was gone, though, I didn't know how to come back."

"None of us blamed you," I said. "Dang, that one year you sold more records than the Beatles."

Glen smiled. "That was quite a year," he said.

"I dug my heels in, as soon as we got to Arkansas," I said. "Those first six years in Arizona felt like a fraud. There was no unpredictable weather. There was no dew on the grass. Well, if you had grass. Most of our neighbors had given up and dumped gravel in their yards. When I got here, I knew I was home."

Glen found a pebble, skipped it across the water. The rock hitting the surface sounded like firecrackers, three loud pops. He frowned. "Those last years were mighty hard. My whole life I'd believed I was on this planet to help folks forget their troubles. At the end, it was as if everybody's troubles were sitting on my chest."

He was talking about the Alzheimer's that chewed him up, that broke his heart. Every day was another subtraction problem until even the sharp-edged light of an August day was an undefinable thing.

"Is it better now?" I asked and pointed to the heavens.

"You can't even imagine," he said.

I blinked hard against the tears that burned my eyes. The day before, I'd come home from the store, put the ice cream in the pantry. I didn't find the carton until after dinner when Carl wanted dessert. It wasn't my first forgetting.

"I'll be sixty soon," I said. "Before the calendar changes from August to September. I was planning a big birthday party, but I've got this daughter I'm crossways with." I rubbed my arms against the damp night. "I don't think I can fix it, and I don't think I could stand having a party without her.

"Carl's going to take me to Western Sizzlin'. I got a friend who offered to take me to the Dolly Parton's Stampede in Branson the next day."

I looked at Glen. He was staring at his hands.

The lake smelled of fish and old leaves. A breeze blew through the trees, the sound like a deck of cards being shuffled. "I lit a candle for you when I heard you'd crossed over," I said.

"Awful nice of you," Glen said.

"When you left this earth, you took a part of my girlhood with you. I grew up with your songs. I kept a poster of you on my bedroom wall."

Glen shook his head, an expert on loss, a Ph.D. in sorrow.

"I forget people's names sometimes," I said. "I took my wedding ring off months ago when I cleaned the oven. Still haven't found it. I couldn't remember the word 'fork' last week. I call my dog by my old dead dog's name about ninety percent of the time."

I could see the raccoons rising, their bodies wobbly as they inched along into the woods. Glen said, "It could be nothing at all, Mary Alice. Just the effects of time, of too many memories."

"I do have a truckload of memories," I said, and relief eased through me.

We lay back on the dock, the damp wood cool, the night electric with crickets and tree frogs. An owl hooted. "I'd have the birthday party if I were you," he said.

I could see the globe of a flashlight on the walking trail a few yards away. I could hear two voices, the high trill of a girl, the bass of a boy. The girl said, "If my mom finds out I snuck away to see you, she'll kill me!" The boy answered, so low I couldn't make out the words.

Glen grinned. "There's nothing new under the sun," he said. "Thank God for that."

I started to mention his own reputation with the ladies, the scandals that followed him like his own shadow for years and years, but something about the easiness of his body made me want to spare him any bad memories.

"I'd better get you back," Glen said and pulled me to my feet. I wondered if the young couple saw us, if they were surprised by the sight of a young man and an old woman on the dock, so close they could be up to something.

Back at home, we sat on the porch, and I asked him to sing "By the Time I Get to Phoenix." I remembered every word.

When he finished, he placed his hands in my hair just above my ears, kissed the top of my head, and took his jacket off and wrapped it around my shoulders. He took a few steps and then turned around. "Have the party," he said again. "Let the people who love you love you."

As he walked away, I pulled the coat tight around me. It smelled like woodsy aftershave and old cigarettes and spilled whiskey. Remnants of another time.

The lights in my neighbor's house flicked on just as the sun started to rise, but I stayed on the porch, watching Glen leave, his hands in his pockets, his head turning now and then, as if he was taking in every fencepost, every blade of grass, every bird on a limb. I tried to look at them the way he did, and suddenly they were the stuff of miracles, they were as precious as newborn lambs.

Summer

A Million Shattered Stars

I was born on a day so hot shingles melted on rooftops, all across town. My mama is telling me this, has told me this a hundred times, and is telling me again because the story shows her at her most valiant, shows her in the kind of pain epidurals were made for, though she didn't mind at all. "Not one bit," she says and licks the tiniest bit of icing from the bakery cake right off her fingers.

The way I would start is this: I was born on the Fourth of July more than three decades ago, which is true and which is today, but this escapes my mama. She has never celebrated Independence Day. She has seen it always as a day that recollects war. She has had enough of war.

Instead, it's this story. The shingles melting, the grass golden in its death, and my daddy passed out in the bedroom in the middle of the afternoon. "You remember our bedroom, Norma Lee. Those wool army blankets over the windows so your daddy could sleep. That's what happens when you work the graveyard shift from midnight until God knows when."

86

Mama likes this part of the story. It takes my daddy out of the picture.

I pick up a blue rose, made entirely of frosting, off the corner of my cake, and plop it in my mouth.

Mama's eyes narrow. "You were such a small baby," she says as if to indicate her displeasure at my size now. She is a narrow woman who eats from my old baby plate to stay that way.

"So I left him in that bed," she says.

I breathe out, tap the table with my fork. None of it stops her. I know she left him there. I know that when he woke and found her gone, he didn't read the note she left on the kitchen table. I know that he headed to Teensie's Bar and Grill on Tupelo Street and drank beer until it was time to go to work.

He didn't meet me until the next afternoon when I was almost an entire day old.

Mama pats my hand. "It's not what killed the marriage," she says. Which is to say, it's exactly what killed the marriage.

My birthday cake has white marshmallow frosting so shiny I can see my reflection. I pick up the knife and slice off another skinny piece.

"Norma Lee," my mama says, her voice heavy with displeasure, which makes me cut off another piece.

"Y'all didn't divorce until I was seven," I say, like an attorney who's just discovered new evidence.

"Wasn't your fault, I told you that."

I hear the first firecracker of the night, just as the sky is darkening. Chance and Chase, the kids next door, are wild for fireworks. Chance, the oldest, who's maybe twelve, yells, "Chase, you dummy, don't light 'em one at a time. Light 'em all up!"

Mama rises, goes to the kitchen window, closes it. "You like to have killed me being born. Doc Patton said I'd never have another child." My mama touches her throat, pushes a stray lock of hair, dyed black as coal, back behind her ear.

I say nothing, so she says, "I only tell you this in case you're thinking of having children of your own."

At thirty-three, with no prospects for love, the thought of children seems like a broken promise.

A bottle rocket screams past the window, lands in the bushes. One of the boys calls out, "You got to shoot 'em in the other direction. Old Mrs. Hannah'll call the cops sure as she'll scratch her own butt," and then laughter erupts.

Mama's face goes red, then white, and then red again.

"They don't mean anything," I say. "Just boys being boys."

"Their mama needs to get control. That youngest one can't be older than six or seven. There is no daddy. Or there's a different daddy for each of them, and neither one is around." Mama waves her hand in front of her face. "I forget which."

I look at the clock. It is almost eight. My birthday will be over in four more hours.

"My own daddy, now he was a fine gentleman. He treated my sweet mama like a queen. The war, though." She is twisting a dishtowel between her hands, turning it into a rope. "He slept with a pistol underneath his pillow. If you got up after everybody had gone to bed, you might get shot. We children understood that. Daddy pulled that pistol on your Grandmama Ethel when she stayed over once. She didn't know the rules. I got up, and there she was in the hall, her hands raised like a bank robber caught by the cops. She was saying, 'Jimmy, it's me. It's your ma. Put the gun down, Jimmy.' She never stayed past dark again."

All across town fireworks are going off, the sky turning into a big color wheel of light and smoke.

"Daddy went to war," I say. "He never talks about it. Not ever."

"You wouldn't want him to."

"He told you, though. Surely he told you."

"By and by," she says. "By and by."

I go stand by the window. Chase and Chance are in their backyard. They've brought out the big guns: Roman candles, towering fountains, cherry bombs. The grass is the color of hay. There is not a mama or daddy in sight.

I watch for a while, but they don't light a thing, just walk around their bounty like kids playing musical chairs, waiting for the song to stop. It is only after I sit down, after I finally turn away, that I hear a boom, and then whooping, and then dead quiet.

"We're going to have to wear earmuffs before this night is over," Mama says.

Not five minutes later, someone is beating on our door so hard it shakes. When I open it, Chase and Chance are standing there, white-faced, sweaty. They point to the fire they've caused. It is licking the air with its long fingers. It is snapping and sparking. Chase starts to cry. Chance croaks out, "Help us." It is more like a whimper.

Mama rushes past them. She's grabbed our jumbo water hose, and she's stretching it as far as she can. I'm right behind her, turning on the faucet. I run back inside and head for the linen closet. On the top shelf are the old army blankets. I grab three. Hand two off to Chase and Chance. We run like Olympians toward the flames and unfurl our blankets. Chase is saying, "Dammit, dammit, dammit," and my mama doesn't even shush him.

We are all water then, and fire, and beaters of the flames. Mama misdirects the hose and soaks the three of us. The flames seem to die down, seem to crouch for a second, but then they catch air and zoom back to life. "We may have to call the fire department," I call out, and the boys both howl. They're thinking they could go to jail, I suspect. They have faces that look like they understand incarceration. I push them behind me with one arm, and Mama keeps spraying.

"All y'all throw your blankets on the fire," she says, and the boys hesitate. She points to three spots where the blankets should go. It doesn't make sense to them, to give up their only weapons on this burning battlefield. "Go on!" she yells, and we do as we're told. The fire reacts, sizzles, smoke rising from the edges. Mama stomps the covers down. She keeps the hose going, all across the thick wool, until they're sopping wet.

Chance and Chase are the kind of forlorn kids you see in ads about hunger. Chance has a skinny face, eyes that are too close together, and dimples that make you forget everything else. Chase has front teeth that overlap, and ears that stick out, and brows that knit together when he talks.

"What were you thinking?" Mama asks, but neither boy answers.

We stand like this for maybe five minutes, vigilant, Chase holding onto Chance's arm. "Let's go inside," Mama says. "If the fire spikes up again, we can be out here in a heartbeat."

Chance and Chase follow us. Their faces glow when they see the cake. I grab towels from the laundry room, and we dry off as best we can.

"We're sorry as sin," Chance says.

90

"You could've killed somebody," Mama says, and then she looks at them and backs off. "It's my daughter's birthday," she says and points at me. "Norma Lee's."

"Sit down," I say. "Help me finish off this cake."

They are happy eaters. They smile with frosting on their teeth. When the phone rings, Mama motions for me to answer it. When I do, I hear Daddy's voice.

"Hey, Honey," he says. "Your mama been telling you about the day you were born?"

"Yep," I say.

"Did she tell you you're not responsible for our divorce?"

"Twice," I say.

The line goes quiet, but then Daddy says, "It really wasn't your fault, Norma Lee." He coughs, inhales, says, "Wasn't her fault, either. Figured it was high time I owned up to that."

The static on the line ricochets between him and me.

"Well, anyway," he finally says. "I wanted to say I love you both."

Mama is wiping Chase's face with the dishtowel, and he is leaning into it like it's the best part of his long, hard day. I've never imagined her the way she was before I came along, the way she was before her heart broke and daddy left, but I imagine it now. I did not ruin her marriage. I did not ruin her life. The war, who knows, maybe the war did it, but who can stop a war?

The city park is having their fireworks show, not a half mile from here. Great spiders of light arc above us, bomb the darkness, rush in through our kitchen window. Mama turns toward me, reaches out and grabs my hand, kisses it, suddenly, as if she's stealing something. I have the telephone in my other hand, my daddy's voice just barely a memory.

Chase and Chance are ready to head back outside. "Come go with us," Chance says, and so we do, the four of us soldiering into the night, past the smoldering blankets, walking beneath a sky that is splintering above us, is coming apart, if you want to know the God's honest truth. But right here, right now, we are held together. We are part of this night of a million shattered stars, fractured, sure, but filled with so much light it hardly seems to matter.

She Broke My Heart and Stole My Wallet

It was blowing up a storm when we started to practice, our bluegrass band called Sweet and Lowdown, but that didn't stop Effie. He thinks you got to play no matter what. If the tornado sirens go off down in town and one of our old ladies calls up here at the hunting cabin we all share, Effie'll say, "Y'all can go get in your fraidy holes if you want to. Me, I'm playing my fiddle."

Well, you can't go to the storm cellar with your tail between your legs, so we stay, me and Layman and King, even though King, who plays the washtub, lost his house in the tornado of '96 and he still shakes when the sky rumbles. And then Effie'll start in on some song like "When the Roll is Called Up Yonder," just to put his spin on how things might turn out if a twister does find us.

So we're playing, me on the guitar, and we're looking out the window, where you can see the sky turning the color of a two-day bruise, and King's sweating and Layman's got his eyes shut like he does when he plays mandolin, and Effie, truth be told, can be a flat-out bully. So he's getting the show list together and acting like everything's business as usual.

"I think we should start with 'Sitting on the Front Porch,'" Effie says. "Crowd pleaser, every single time. And then 'Baby's Little Shoes.' And then 'Walking with Clementine' for the old folks. We'll finish with 'God Bless the U.S.A,' since the veterans' home is bringing a bus."

Lightning is hitting closer, the sky like the Fourth of July. King's sat down and he's turned white as milk, and the sight of it causes my own heart to tremble. King's a big man. He can't even button his overalls up all the way on the side, so when he doubles over and then falls out of his chair, none of us knows what to do.

"I ain't doing no mouth-to-mouth," Effie says, while the rest of us are trying to set King up.

King comes to soon enough, and he leans up on his elbow, looking like ten miles of bad road. And just then, the hail starts, and it sounds like gunfire when it hits the tin roof.

"My new truck," King says and covers his eyes.

Our pickups are parked outside, and they're getting blasted. I see my old Dodge, the one I've had since Mae left me in '81. The hail, big as cotton bolls, is hitting it, and it makes me sick to death.

Effie's truck, his is under the old lean-to car porch we threw up last summer. Well, sure it is, I think.

Then Layman, who's usually as peaceful as a Sunday morning, yells, "Damn it to hell," and hits the wall with his fist. We all go quiet. We ain't seen nothing like this before, and it feels like the storm is moving inside with us.

Outside, the rain flashes down. Pounding everything, soaking through what used to be my back windshield.

"Mercy sakes alive," is all I can say.

King tries to stand, grabbing my arm to do it. He's about as wide as he is tall, and he near about pulls me down on his way up.

"I'm off like a prom dress," King says, "so don't try to stop me." But then he stands still for a second and pulls himself up as tall as he can like he does when a pretty woman walks by on the avenue. He's trying to push his chest out farther than his belly, which ain't no easy task.

"You're about as helpful as the U.S. Congress," he says to Effie. "We should send you to Washington, D.C., where you could bow up like a mad dog every time somebody has a good idea, and then vote against it."

We don't talk politics, not since we got into a knockdown drag-out when Clinton ran for governor that second time, but King don't seem to be abiding by any rules today. I take a step toward him, in case I need to referee. King just keeps going.

"You act mighty high like you're the backbone of Sweet and Lowdown," King says. He points to Layman. "But Layman here, he might not play as good as you like, but he's the one got the news folks out here to do that story calling us the best bluegrass band in Arkansas. And he books every show, and when you get drunk, let's just be honest here, when you get drunk, you can't play worth a dang."

Effie's a little banty rooster of a man, but he's been known to fight mean, and when he lunges at King, it takes me and Layman to stop him.

We're holding Effie by his scrawny arms, and he's kicking, his cowboy boots flying off the wood floor.

"You are a liar and a snake, King Brammel," Effie says. "A liar and a snake. You're going to go straight to hell. And just so you know, when you do, I plan to play the fiddle on your grave."

King looks like he could put Effie in the ground right then and there his own self. I start to butt in, but then Layman steps in, which is hard for him, I know because he don't like fighting.

"Y'all cut it out," Layman says. "Ain't nobody going to hell, Effie," he says and then points right at him, "you and King need to quit showing your behinds. That gig on Saturday pays a hundred dollars, plus they feed us. We ain't had a set-up like that since we played that Blue Magnolia shindig for the rich ladies who wanted to dress up in thousand-boots and wear tight jeans and drink beer in front of their husbands."

And then Layman swells up like I never seen him do before. "And Effie, we ain't playing 'Walking with Clementine,'" he says. "The old folks can do without it for one dang night. I wrote my own song, and I want to sing it. It's called 'She Broke My Heart and Stole My Wallet.'"

I'd known Layman forty-two years, and that was the first I'd heard of his songwriting. His ex-girlfriend, the one who brought over the Mexican casserole when Layman's wife died two years ago, was probably the inspiration for this new tune. Word was, she was over in Branson now, hooked up with a cowboy singer who wore a bolo tie and colored his hair.

Effie's face is scarlet. Even his ears are red. He looks like he might ignite at any minute. But he backs down soon enough, his shoulders falling. He looks at all of us, me and King and Layman, and then he says, "Fine, that's fine as a feather. I been carrying you yahoos for way too long."

King is towering over Effie, and for a minute he looks like he don't know what to do. He eyes me and then Layman, then shakes his head.

The wind is still howling, and the windows rattle. Finally, he cuffs Effie on the shoulder, and then the two shake hands, and the rain keeps falling, and the wind whistles down the chimney.

Effie has a bottle in his fiddle case, and he goes to get it. "Ain't nobody driving till the rain stops," he says. "And that includes you, King."

And then we sit down and pass the bottle until Layman starts singing. "I loved a girl from Minnesota. Loved her with a passion true. And then she stole my dadburn wallet, took it out and followed you. You must be a handsome cowboy. You must look like Johnny Cash. But my friend, you Dandy Heartthrob, I forewarn you, she is fishing for your stash."

We are laughing now. Effie brings out his fiddle, and I pick up my guitar, and Layman his mandolin. King drags out the washtub, and we get back at it, the boys from Sweet and Lowdown, and we start to play, better than we have in a long time, maybe better than we ever will again.

Sometimes You Forget

I wake alone this morning, my husband already off to work, a note on my nightstand scribbled in haste. My husband works as a diesel mechanic at a trucking company, and someone called in sick, so he left our bed while I was dreaming of my old lover, a man I nearly married. In my dream I was saying, "I do love you. I'll always love you. I just can't be with you anymore."

Which is almost an exact transcription of our actual breakup almost three years ago.

I am tangled in the bedclothes now, the blue sheets and the white comforter, and when I get up there are our two schnauzers, Happy and Mr. Wigglesworth, waiting for me, their stub tails wagging like tiny windshield wipers.

Outside, the hens wait. Ulysses, Gilead, Velta, Madge, and Honey. They call to me from inside their house, anxious little birds, and when I open their door to their chicken coop, they stumble down the walkway that leads to their freedom, like drunken pirates on a gangplank.

The sky has gone pink, off to the west, and hawks are in the hayfield that adjoins our yard, swooping so low they cast a shadow across me. I used to love the hawks, before I got chicks, and now I only think: chicken killer, chicken killer, chicken killer.

There is a rhythm to the morning. I feed the dogs. I feed the chickens. And then I make tea and toast. I love the feel of an ordinary morning, the necessary adjustments of everyday life.

But this morning, the dream is troubling me. The man I broke up with, his name was Sam. He used to cook for me on Friday nights, complicated dishes that took thought and planning, and he'd pour wine, and he'd draw a bubble bath for me—I always arrived disheveled, straight from work at the vet's office—while I waited for dinner and he played Schubert from an old record player he'd restored bit by bit. He hummed while he cooked. That is what I remember.

On the drive home, I'd listen to Trisha Yearwood, and Mary Chapin Carpenter and Roseanne Cash. I'd stop at the store and get a Mountain Dew and drink it fast, ready for the jolt of caffeine, because I always felt like I was in a fog when I left.

Sam had a way about him, a kind of introspection that made you stop and look at your own life. And when I looked at mine, I realized I was false when I was with him. I read what he read, dusty books from used bookstores. Zen and the Art of Motorcycle Maintenance stands out. Sonnets from the Portuguese. The Heart is a Lonely Hunter.

We went to piano bars. We listened to NPR. Even on hikes, he'd teach me the names of flowers, tell me the complicated history of Arkansas. And I would sneak candy from my pockets and think about the hotel room that was waiting. The hot tub. Room service. HBO.

When I broke up with Sam, I had to take off the engagement
ring he'd given me, the biggest diamond I'd ever owned. I slipped
it into his hand, and he would not close his fingers around it. He
looked astounded, his forehead creased, his black hair shiny as he
shook his head in disbelief. He was the far better catch than I
would ever be, and we both knew it.

"Jeannie," he said. "I hope you find what makes you happy."
And he meant it. That's how good he was.

There are whole days when I don't think about Sam. Some
nights, though, as my husband sleeps, I imagine what it would be
like to have two lives. One in the here and now, sitting as I am on
the porch swing as the chickens run by. And one where I would
have been raised differently, somewhere other than a trailer, by
parents who talked to me about the future, who made me feel
equal to a man like Sam.

This is not fair to my husband. I think we can all agree on
that.

The phone is ringing in the kitchen, and so I rise and go
inside. My husband is calling to make sure I let the chickens out.
"Sometimes you forget," he says, but there was only the one time,
and I sigh into the phone.

What makes a good wife good? If you look at my record, I
would qualify. My husband's clothes are clean. Supper's on the
table at six o'clock sharp every evening. Last night he said, "You
know what rednecks call a seven-course meal?" And when I said
no, he answered, "A six pack of Bud and a possum," and I laughed
like I meant it.

Well, maybe I did.

I am making pork tenderloin tonight. I am making deviled
eggs and vegetable whip, a recipe my mother-in-law gave me

when we got married. Carrots, potatoes, onion, an apple. In the kitchen, Happy and Mr. Wigglesworth are begging for treats, their bodies jiggly with excitement. I get out two milk bones and make them shake and then roll over before I dole out the treats.

There are candles in the cabinet above the sink, and I am standing on a stool trying to reach them. The thought of candlelight came to me in a flash, a kind of penance for my divided heart, and I open the doors and rummage until I find them. In the cabinet is also a notebook, plain as notebooks go, but one I've never seen. I take it down and sit at the kitchen table as I leaf through the pages.

It is filled with my husband's lists. Things like the names of paint colors we've used on walls, construction estimates for the sun porch we've been talking about building, dates he's changed the oil in my car. There is a tab sticking out, and on it he's written "Goals." I flip the page. He wants to save five hundred dollars this year, run a 5K, and visit his mother more. There are steps to each goal, even the visits to his mom. (Take her to lunch every payday.) I turn the page again, and then I read, "Get Jeannie to love me." There are no steps listed. Just a big question mark.

I feel my face grow hot. I close the book. I think about the day he asked me to marry him. He brought me flowers. Daisies. And he didn't have a ring. "I want you to get what you want," he said, after I'd said yes. That night we went to the mall, and he was holding my hand so tight it hurt. He was smiling like a kid does. That open smile that sees nothing but good coming down the road, even when the road twists and turns so much you can't see the end of it.

I look around my kitchen, the living room beyond. It looks

every bit like a home, right down to the big wooden monogram above the fireplace, but I guess it really isn't. The timer on the oven sounds, a sharp beep that makes me jump. Happy and Mr. Wigglesworth howl, and I rise slowly to shut the timer off.

I change out of my yoga pants and T-shirt. I put on perfume and let my hair fall loose around my shoulders. I dig out the stash of cards Sam sent me during our courtship from under the bed. I go outside and make a fire in the backyard.

I don't read one card. I don't run my finger across the fine script of my name. I stand so close to the fire that there will be smoke on my clothes when my husband comes home. The hens come to watch the memories burn. Ulysses struts around the edges of the fire, leading the other ladies like a warmonger general marching to battle.

When my husband sits at the table, I scoot my chair next to his, our thighs touching. "What's going on?" he asks. And I say, "Can't a woman love her husband without being questioned?"

He smiles, and when he looks at me, the heat rises. Later, I explore his body. I have always loved the bodies of men, their secret soft places, the scent of hard work, the taste of salt. My husband has beautiful hands. Muscled limbs. A flat stomach.

An image of Sam flashes. In bed, he would ask, "Do you like this?" "How does this feel?" "Do you know what you do to me?" I'd answer with a moan, by closing my eyes, by arching my back.

My husband is all action. His mouth and body say it all. Now though, he seems to understand I have drifted, so he shifts, and suddenly I am beneath him. And then, he speaks. "You are mine," he says, more of a question than a claim.

"I am yours," I say. "I am yours."

There are no other words for quite a while. For so long that when we finally speak, our throats are dry, our voices scratchy. We walk to the kitchen our hands linked, Happy and Mr. Wigglesworth at our heels. There, we drink our fill from glasses made from sand and forged by fire.

One Summer in Judsonia

Decades ago, in the summer of my twenty-second year, just as the corn and tomatoes were coming to life, a man found his way to me. He was driving a gold and brown Ford LTD. He was wearing polyester pants the color of carrots. He was listening to music that rang from his stereo, louder than any alarm in town.

All I knew at that time was that he was an intruder and that I was not dressed for company. I had on overalls with a T-shirt underneath and work boots, grimy from a long day's work. My hair was a tumble of brown curls pinned loosely on top of my head. I smelled like sweat and new-mown grass.

He was selling leather-bound classics: Ulysses, Moby Dick, Elizabeth Barrett Browning's Sonnets from the Portuguese. He carried Ulysses under his arm. The volume had seen better days. I doubted he had access to an entire set, even if I had given him the check he wanted, and at first sight he didn't seem to be a reader, or at least he never quoted a passage to me. I let him sit on my porch, but I kept my hoe in my hand, a warning sharp as a snake's tongue, in case he got any ideas. He asked after my husband, and

I laughed. I intended never to marry, but how could he know that? It was 1972, and most women over eighteen had walked the aisle by then. I could see his response, that moment of surprise when he looked around, admiring the place, I believe. It was a fine property. A two-story house, forty-four acres. A red barn. Holstein cattle in the field.

"Yes," I said. "It's all mine," although he hadn't actually asked.

"I live in my car," he said and pointed to the LTD. "Before that, I lived in Ybor City in Florida."

He didn't have the manners of a traveling salesman, which is to say he wasn't especially charming, or quick, or fast-talking. He was twenty-seven, I learned later, a veteran of the Vietnam War, and he had the look of someone lost, or maybe of someone not wanting to be found. He had a scar that ran around his right thumb. He had shaggy, barely brown hair that he kept pushing behind his ears. He looked a lot like Robert Redford, whose movies I adored.

"I've never lived anywhere but here in Judsonia. My parents," I said, and then stopped. I didn't talk about them with outsiders. They'd trekked to the Alaskan wilderness and decided to disappear. I was supposed to go with them, but I'd gotten a summer job at Bennie's Eating Emporium the year I graduated high school and waved them off when they said they might not come back. They sent back one letter. One! In it, they gave me the farm.

His name was Winston Shockley. He'd never been to Arkansas before. He smiled when I asked him why, and then he sang a line from "Never Been to Spain," a Three Dog Night hit that was all the rage. He'd been to Oklahoma, he sang, and for some reason, I laughed. His voice was a perfect baritone. He had little gold hairs on his arms. His eyes were the blue of heaven.

I put him up in the barn that night. It was foolhardy, and I knew it. Getting undressed for bed, I felt embarrassed, even though there were walls between us, curtains, doors, a quarter acre, a barn door solid as the night.

The next morning, I walked to the barn and knocked tentatively. I invited him to eat with me. His hands swallowed the coffee mug. I liked his elbows on the table, his eyes scanning the newspaper, his eyes scanning me when he thought I was busy at the stove.

A truckload of day workers showed up, mostly high school kids from town, a few old men who'd worked for my parents. I directed them to the cornfield and put Charlie, the oldest of the men, in charge. He scratched his head and said, "You feeling poorly, Miss Emmaline?" I never missed work. I assured him all was well, and turned back to the house, to Winston, who was still at the kitchen table.

We spent most of the day at Monroe Lake. He could float on his back for a solid hour; I'd never seen anything like it. He could read while he did it, and showed me so, the front page of the local paper soggy by the time he finished. I sat in an inner tube and watched him, transfixed.

"You started to tell me about your parents yesterday," he said finally, when he'd grown tired of floating and began to tread water.

"Ah, well," I said. "It's not a good story for a summer day."

"Well, I'm sorry, all the same. For whatever happened," he said.

I opened my mouth but didn't speak. He assumed they were dead. For all I knew, they were. I paddled closer to him. "What are your parents like?"

"My mother is small and round and happy," he said. "My father is tall and thin and angry."

"What was the war like?"

He splashed water with the palm of his hand. "Not a story for a summer day," he said. "Why aren't you married?" he asked, without missing a beat.

"I don't believe in marriage," I said, as defiant as I could manage in the presence of a man I feared had the power to change my mind.

"Are you into free love?"

I laughed again. "Nothing on this green earth is free." And then I said, "Why aren't you married?"

"Not enough room in the LTD," he said, and laughed again.

I might not have loved him if he'd left that day, but he did not. By the end of the week, he was working beside me in the fields. On Saturday, he drove to town, came back with a loaf of French bread, two bottles of Boone's Farm, two steaks he grilled without wearing his shirt.

It was not as if I'd never been pursued by a man. I had. Sometimes I'd been caught. But I always found my way home again. With Winston, it was as if he was not in pursuit at all. He was easy like breathing is easy. I dressed carefully that night, put on a yellow sundress, let my hair down, rubbed baby oil on my legs.

He found my dad's old albums and put Etta James on the stereo. He poured cheap wine and sat on the arm of my chair while we drank it. When "At Last" began to play, he pulled me to my feet, and we danced in the living room while the last of the light streamed through the tall windows.

There is something solid in some men that makes a woman believe she can be soft. Winston had that. His arms around me felt like the rails of a fence that keeps every good thing safe. His chin, on the top of my head, felt like a promise. All manner of things happened next, and all manner of clothing fell in a trail, all the way to my childhood bed.

Before he left, he said, "I want you to know, Emmaline, that I could get used to this."

The next day we walked through the pear orchard my grandfather planted in the 1940s, and Winston despaired at the condition it was in. We drove to the county extension office, and the agent talked to us for an hour, telling us how to save the trees that were left, how to get the pears to produce again.

We worked the orchard together, and one day he asked for two hundred dollars for irrigation equipment. It rang false when he said it, and I thought for a minute that he was conning me, and I didn't like the way that made me feel. I made some excuse, and he didn't ask again. He carried water to the trees through all of July. In August, he stopped trying.

One September afternoon, just as the heat of summer was ratcheting down from hellfire-fury to simply unbearable, Winston began to drift. He spent an entire Sunday morning washing and waxing his LTD. He brought a map into the house and circled the state of Colorado. "Have you ever snow skied?" he asked, offhandedly, as if my answer didn't matter. I thought of my mother and father, the winter and spring they spent bent over a map of Alaska. I thought about how snow blinds you, burns you, disorients you. "No," I said.

Winston was so caught up tracing the red and blue lines with his finger that he didn't seem to hear me. "Are you leaving?" I asked, and he told me he was, the very next morning.

The barn seemed as far away as the east is from the west that night. I paced across my bedroom floor, wondering what to do, wondering why I was so easy to leave. I believed then, and I believe it still, that he expected me to go to him, to make things right, as I suppose most women would have done. But there was something in me that would not allow me to give a man the upper hand.

When he left, I was stoic. I sent along fried chicken, a jug of tea, peach cobbler. I imagined Winston turning around, a cloud of red dirt following him down my rutted road, but that did not happen, not that day or any other. Not in all these years.

But then, last week, just as the sun was setting, a UPS truck pulled down the lane. I opened the door to see it, and my old dog, Bessie, stood beside me and howled. The young driver handed me a box that I took inside and opened slowly. There was no return address. Inside was a tattered copy of Ulysses and a note from Winston, who is now a widower and a grandfather and works part time at a Best Buy in Kansas.

I have read his note so many times; I could recite it to you now. "Dear Emmaline," it begins, "I have carried you with me every day since that summer. Sometimes you were as heavy as all the books I carried back then. Other times, you were as light as the breeze that blew across our skin on that first night in your narrow bed."

There are days when I think he's saying he loved me then and loves me still, and that he's paving his way to return to me. There are days when I read it and think it's a goodbye note, that he must be dying.

It is such a small token, so late in the game, it shouldn't

matter. But time has a way of blurring the past until it looks like one of Monet's fuzzy paintings. Holding it in my hands, though, I can summon up that time, the sun on my bare shoulders, Winston's hand on the small of my back. I can see myself at twenty-two, as beautiful as I would ever be, my body almost perfect, and Etta James singing in the background, telling me my lonely days were finally, thankfully over, and I believed her, even if none of it was ever true.

Struck

My mama has been hit by lightning, so my tore-up leg holds little interest to her. "Go wash," is all she says when I stumble through the front door, still shaky from the experience, a bandana wrapped around the gash.

When I return from work, she's sitting at the kitchen table. Peaches are scattered across the countertops. Her intention, she said when I left that morning, was to make jam. It 3:30, and still the peaches remain, reminders of my mama's sloth.

"What happened to your leg?" she asks, eight hours late in my opinion, and then dips a carrot into a bowl of onion dip.

"I was climbing through the barbed wire fence." I wait, but she doesn't answer. "I slipped," I say. It had taken six Band-Aids to cover the wound.

"Not very smart," she says. "The gate's not locked. Foolish not to use it."

"Still," I say.

"I couldn't sleep again last night," she says finally. "Dreams."

And I ask, "The lightning?"

"Always."

It's been eleven months since the storm tore through. She was in the tin lean-to where we keep the riding mower. When the lightning struck, Mama was leaning against the shed, and it grabbed her like a miser holds a dollar bill. Her mutt dog Jester was with her, and he watched as my mama lit up. He watched until he couldn't stand it and then he backed up and ran straight to her.

Jester died when the electricity jumped from her to him.

My mama did not.

She wishes she had.

Our neighbor found her and called the ambulance. We buried Jester under the oak tree by the creek as soon as the rain stopped.

My mama's right eye is twitching—a residual effect of the strike. She's still a beautiful woman. Go to town with her, and men will knock you down to shake her hand, to have the chance that she'll smile at them the way she can when she's feeling it.

But the twitching is a problem. The dreams are a problem. The medical bills are a problem.

"I'm having a stone made for Jester," she finally says.

The next morning, the cut, four jagged inches straight down my shin, is gaping. I need stitches, I know I do, but there's no way I'll ask. I wrap up my leg and head to work. I count semis that drive by on the old quarry road. The county's doing a study about road use, and I'm their newest employee. I wear an orange vest and sit in a tan outbuilding. Sometimes I read when I work, so the count is off. I jack it up before I leave at 2:30. Not much, I don't want to get caught, but enough so it seems like I pay attention.

"How's your mama?" Theron says to me when he brings me

lunch.

"She's having a stone made for Jester."

Theron shakes his head. He looks like John Wayne. "John-Wayne-on-a-Brush Hog," is what Mama calls him because he clears land for a living. "Granite?" he asks.

"I guess. Or gold," I say. "Sure loved that dog."

"Gave up his life for her," Theron says. "No greater love—"

"Couldn't get Daddy to do so much as take out the trash."

Theron rubs my shoulders. He didn't know my daddy.

A semi passes, and I watch. "Write it down," Theron says, so I reach for my notebook and put another X on the paper.

Mama is sitting on the porch when I get home. Her left foot is on the railing. She's painting her toenails pink. "I'm gonna have the stone say, 'Jester—Hero, Friend, Soul Mate, Defender.'"

It's 101 today, but Mama's not sweating. It's another thing she gave up when the lightning struck. To get cool, she has to lie down on the cold bathroom tile, get her skin right up against it, like a dog does. "I got fried and now I can't perspire," Mama said, the first time I found her curled up by the commode.

"Soul mate sounds like you were in love with Jester," I say.

"I wish you'd shut up," she says and storms off, walking on her heels, her toenails pointing toward heaven.

When the stone comes in, Jester is misspelled. It reads: Hester. And my mama cries.

I go to the kitchen. More peaches have fallen from the trees that line our fencerow. Mama's picked them up again, scattered them across the counters, piled them on the living room floor next to her chair. I pick one up, wash it off and take a bite.

All night long I peel and cube. I open freezer bags and toss in handfuls of peaches. At two in the morning, I've had my fill. The floor is sticky, the sink cluttered with peelings, the freezer full. I take the rest of the peaches and put them in grocery sacks. The next morning, I leave them by the road with a sign that reads, "Be a Peach. Take a Peach."

For weeks Jester's stone sits on the coffee table. Mama touches it when she walks by. Glides her hand along the smooth gray top. Traces the letters with her fingertip. She starts buying flowers in town, daisies and carnations, and she places them on the stone where neither Jester nor Hester lies.

"He was a good dog," Mama says one Sunday afternoon. "Looked at me like he knew things a dog had no business knowing."

"He was a good dog," I say. "The best dog."

On Monday, the doctor released Mama to go back to her job at Ace Comb Company, but she's been resisting, and now HR is involved. On the phone, she says, "Well, for one thing I can tell when a phone's about to ring. I can feel it about to ring. My heart jumps around in my chest, my hearing's gone all tinny. I can't sweat, for heaven's sake." She is thumping her chest now. She is crying now. "At the Sonic," she says, "when I press the red button to order, their whole intercom system shuts down." She waits. "It certainly does. I have been banned from Happy Hour! Go ask the manager!"

I call in sick the next day. I call Theron, who rumbles down the path to our house in his yellow pickup. His window is rolled down, and he has a brown hand towel laying across the doorframe so that he can hang his arm out and not get burned.

"Joetta," he says when he sees me. "My Joetta."

"Get me out of here," I say.

"One minute," he says, and heads into the house.

He comes out with Jester's stone. "We gotta fix it. None of this business is gonna stop until we do."

And so we fly down the highway, me and Theron and Jester/Hester's stone. We weave through Summitville, we climb the hill to Hiland, and we find a stonemason who agrees to help.

When we get home, Mama's in the yard waiting, her arms folded across her chest.

"You took my stone," she says.

"And we brought it back, Cissy," Theron says. "See," he says, and he unwraps the granite.

I have never seen my mama cry like she does now. She is a river turned wrong side out. Theron hands me the stone and helps her inside.

"Only thing I ever did right was Jester. Not Joetta. No sir, not Joetta. I have failed Joetta."

"Mama," I say. "Stop." But she keeps going.

"Jester, though, now that I did right. Got all his shots. Bought the name-brand food. Washed him every Saturday. He'd stand by my door in the morning. Never barked. Just stood there, waiting.

"I was low that day. I get low a lot. I was thinking about moving away. I always liked the thought of Vermont. I could see me there, nobody knowing me. I'd wear my hair down more. I'd buy sweaters. I'd eat a lobster and chowder and rhubarb, whatever that is.

"Jester was whining. Dogs know storms. I shooed him away. 'Go on home,' I said, and his big ole ears dropped. Nothing sadder than a sad dog. But he wouldn't leave me. Not Jester."

I pull Mama to me. "It's okay," I say. "It's okay."

Theron got us all to sit down. "There are some things in this world worth crumbling over," Theron says, his voice as serious as an undertaker. "War, kids without clean drinking water, the Razorbacks losing."

Mama blew her nose. "Your best friend dying," she says.

"But Jester wouldn't want this, Cissy," Theron says, and then he reaches out and touches her shoulder. "He'd want you to go back to work or go to Vermont or throw an Avon party. Anything but what you're doing now. It'd break his heart to see you like this."

"I can't sweat anymore," Mama says.

"Not a lot of sweating in Vermont," Theron says.

"I can tell when phones are about to ring."

"Might come in handy. They might hire you to troubleshoot at the movie house or something. Stop cell phones before they chime in."

"I can't go to Sonic."

"Not any Sonics in Vermont," Theron says.

"No?" Mama says.

"I don't believe so."

We place the stone on Jester's grave just as the sun sets. Mama says, "You were a good dog, a fine friend, and I never once deserved you. If I could lie down and you could rise up, I'd do it in a minute."

Theron nudged Mama with his elbow. "Cissy," he says, "say something with some truck to it."

Mama takes in air. She stands up taller. "I loved the way you slid across the kitchen floor, sideways, when I called you to eat. I loved the way you pushed against me on the couch, like I was a boulder that couldn't be moved. I loved that you were smarter than people gave you credit for."

Mama hesitates, then takes the clip from her hair and lets it fall. It is a small thing, but it is something to see. Her dark hair rushing down, unleashed, the dappled light beneath the oak, the creek water stumbling along. She takes a step, turns back once to look at the stone, but only for a second, and then we head for home.

Soon, in a day or two, in a week or two, Mama will have to make a decision. The Ace Comb Company won't wait forever for her to come back. She could stay, or she could leave me for Vermont. Theron puts his hand on my neck, right where my ponytail meets my shirt collar. I turn into him. I feel a thousand different things all at once, and he seems to know it. He holds me in the open field as Mama walks ahead, and then he kneels down, he kisses my bandaged shin. "Let's go get that looked at," he says, and I start to cry, and he tells me it's OK, and I start to believe that it just might be.

Past the End of Everything

This was years ago when we lived in the apartment that was so small, I gave you the only bedroom, when I slept on the divan in the living room.

Your daddy and I had been divorced three years by then, and you were only six. I figured you didn't remember me and your daddy together in any real way, but sometimes when you'd come home from his house, your little boy hand in his, you'd pull him through the doorway and you'd say, "Stay!" and I'd wonder what you were thinking.

I still loved that man. But we were fire and gasoline together, or fire and a nuclear reactor, and he later married that woman with the big black hair and too much eyeliner. We both know what a disaster that was.

The night I'm thinking about, you had on your pajamas with the robots on them. And I had on gray sweatpants and one of your dad's T-shirts I'd kept for some reason. We were watching on our VCR *The Great Outdoors* with John Candy, a Canadian we both loved, and we were laughing when he came through the door of the cabin with the grizzly chasing him, and he was trying to tell his family a bear was right behind him, over and over, the words sputtering out, his eyes as big as two pizza pies.

You still had dimples where your knuckles should have shown, a baby's hands. You were eating crunchy lemon cookies that had the circle cut out in the middle. You'd put one on your index finger, twirl it around, take a bite, laugh. It never got old.

When I put you to bed, you smelled like bubble gum flavored toothpaste. You slept with a ratty old bunny, and a He-Man doll from that cartoon you loved.

Sometime in the night, you woke from a bad dream. And then I woke to find you standing over me, your eyes rimmed in red, your soft brown hair standing on end—you pulled your hair back then when things got out of hand—so I knew you'd been despairing for a while.

"Mama," you said and held your arms straight out, and I sat up and lifted you onto the divan, and I placed my hand on the crown of your head. "It's all right, Bobby Boy," I said. "Mama's here."

You were trembling, your little round belly shaking. "I saw all the way to the end," you said.

It was such an odd thing to say. "The end of what?" I asked, and you jabbed your chest and then mine, and you said, "Of us."

I kissed the top of your head. "There's no end to us, baby. You and me, we go on and on. You can't get rid of your mama."

You exhaled, the power of that effort shuddered through your thin chest. "But I saw it."

"A dream, baby doll. Nothing more."

"You promise?"

"I double-dog promise," I said, and you looked at me for a long time, puzzling something out. "Okay," you finally said, and

119

you leaned into me the way you used to do, letting go, letting me hold you up.

A better mama might have asked you more about the dream, but I didn't want to know. I had an imagination myself, and I could see a hundred ways we could end, most of them involving car crashes or house fires. I did wonder, though, if your daddy had been talking to you about how I walked out on him, how he didn't see it coming, although, let me tell you, he dang sure should have.

Maybe in your dream, we'd both gotten eaten by John Candy's grizzly. I did stop playing that movie except in the daylight hours. Before it started, I'd tell you the bear was not a real one, which I believed took a little bit away from John Candy's performance, a thing I hated for you.

I've been thinking about our apartment. It had green shag carpet, a gold sink in the kitchen, a patio door that led to the sorriest little patio I'd ever seen. It cost me three-fourths of my paycheck to rent it, and still, there was no bedroom for me, so I slept on the couch. I'd wake with my back hurting, my neck sore. It was a small thing, and I don't regret it.

Your daddy called me today, something he hasn't done in years. It was a shock to hear his voice. I always thought he sounded like a radio preacher when he was younger. Now he sounds like a gunslinger in those old Westerns he loves so much.

Still, it stirred something in me. The heart doesn't make a lick of sense. He said, "Remember when Bobby was just a itty-bitty thing? How he wouldn't go to sleep without you singing 'Take It Easy' to him." He laughed, and I could just about see his eyes closing as he did it, the color blooming across his cheeks. "Why in the hell did you sing him a song about a man so overrun by womenfolk that he had to hit the road?"

I said, "I liked the part about Winslow, Arizona," I said. "I'd been there as a girl. I'd been all over the state of Arizona before we moved to Arkansas."

Your daddy said, "I can't believe Bobby turned out as good as he did."

Honey, that's what your daddy really thinks about you. He thinks you're good. I know he doesn't say it to you much, or maybe ever. I know you think he's a sorry so-and-so about half the time, but he's not all bad.

There was this one time, long before you were born when your daddy and me were out on the dance floor. I was wearing jeans and high-heeled sandals and a wreath in my hair that I'd woven from honeysuckle I'd found on the fencerow at my house. My hair was the softest brown, just like yours, and I wore it to my waist. Your daddy led me around that dance floor like he was the Pied Piper.

At the end of the night, he said, "You really should stay away from the likes of me." He had his fingers hooked through the belt loops on my jeans. I couldn't have stayed away from him if he'd called a Greyhound bus to carry me off. "I got demons that haunt," he said, and he looked away, frowning.

Turns out, honey, he didn't have any more demons than I did. You get to be a certain age, after having done certain things, and those demons show up on your doorstep with a suitcase in their hands.

They're not really demons, though. They're just regrets we dress up and let move in. I've been working through mine, an old woman finally taking inventory of her life.

That night you woke me up with your dream, I'd been feeling

awful sorry for myself. I was a young woman, younger than you are now. Some of my girlfriends were still going out on Saturday nights, still getting the attention of men who had the power to make their lives easier if they wanted to.

And there I was. Broken and broke. I turned off the TV after you went to bed. Upstairs, the McCarrons were fighting again, and I heard glass shattering as one or the other threw something that hit the wall or floor. I covered my head with my pillow.

I'd gotten everything wrong, I could see that, from marrying your daddy on. And you were going to pay for it right along with me, scraping by week after week. When you stood over me that night, your hair a spiky crown on your perfect head, I'd felt you before I saw you. And then you spoke. "Mama," you said. "I saw all the way to the end."

The next weekend, when you were at your daddy's, I turned that sentence over and over, taking it with me to the market and the second-hand store, to the day-old bread shop where I stocked up on stale snack cakes and yeast rolls just about to go bad.

When you came home on Sunday, I showed you the tidied kitchen, the patio I'd washed down until it sparkled. In your bedroom, I'd hung our old Christmas lights, and the colors danced across the white walls.

My intention was to spruce it up the best I could, to move our lives as far from the end of the road as I could. You put your hands to your mouth when you saw your room, and you jumped up and down. I could have stood in the light from your joy all night long.

Lately, son, I've been seeing all the way to the end, just like you did when you were six, and this time I can't do anything to stop it. I wanted to tell you that, how some days my heart flip-flops in a way that seems dangerous. I get winded working in the yard, tending the flowers, say, or running the push mower. At night, when I should sleep, I figure out how many days I've lived. How many I might have left.

I feel like John Candy in that movie, with a big ole bear behind me. The grizzly's gaining ground, no doubt he is, and I'm looking for a safe place to hide. John Candy ran straight for his cabin, but my refuge is a shabby apartment I can still see in my mind, with shaggy carpet and a son who ate lemon cookies that spun like tops on his little finger.

When your daddy called a little bit ago, he said, "Ellie, I believe we could have made it if you hadn't been so damn stubborn." He's wrong of course, but it's nice to hear.

Now, Bobby, he's headed your way right now and should be there by next Thursday. He wanted to surprise you, but some things are more shock than surprise, so I wanted you to know. I hope when he knocks at your door, you'll open your arms to him. My stubbornness runs deep in you, son, but you're smarter than me by a long shot.

That's it. That's all your old mama wanted to say. That, and thank you. I don't know what would have happened to me if you hadn't come along when you did. You were the piece of heaven I didn't deserve but got anyway. You were the love that took me past the end of everything.

Calling Out the Moon

On the day I said goodbye to Kenner, we saw a girl we'd gone to high school with, who still wore pants so tight you could almost see paradise. "Some things don't never change," Kenner said, and then he waved her over to our table at the Earl's down on Main Street. She had hair the color of apricots. She had rings on her thumbs. She looked like something you'd see at the circus is what I thought, but Kenner told her she looked foxy, and she smiled and fluttered her eyelashes. And after we said our farewells and left the diner, we saw a screech owl in a tree in broad daylight, its wings spread out even though it didn't attempt to fly.

We'd both signed on to Social Security by then, and we'd stand in line at the post office in Booneville on the first day of the month, waiting for the clerk to hand over the checks we'd earned from backbreaking work that had stooped us over and gnarled our hands.

Kenner had an old Chevy truck with a spidery break in the windshield, a buckled tailgate, and I was driving it. My eyes were just a little bit better than his, and as we climbed in, he said, "Don't take me home just yet, Bird." And I said, "Got nowhere to be, Kenner. I'll go anywhere you want."

The truth was, my wife, Ocie, expected me back. She wanted to go to the picture show to see a movie about a dog that had supernatural powers. I said, "Let me make one call," and pulled out my cell phone, big as my wallet, and gave Ocie the news. She called me a name I deserved to be called and then hung up.

Me and Kenner drove past the grade school where we met. "You remember Mrs. Woodruff, in first grade?" Kenner asked. And I told him I did.

"I sat on her lap one day when I was burnt up with fever," Kenner said. "She took me home in her car at lunchtime, and my mama liked to have stroked out because the house was a mess like it always was. Too many kids to take care of and Daddy always gone. Mrs. Woodruff smelled like rose petals on a spring morning. I thought she was the prettiest woman I ever saw."

"It was that red hair," I said. "And the starched white blouses. Our mamas never dressed like that."

"You remember that time we tied Miss Measles to her chair when she fell asleep? We were in fifth grade." Kenner said, and he laughed, his belly rolling when he did. "I took a licking for that, Bird, but I'd do it again just to see her face when she woke up."

"We both took a licking for that, Kenner, as I recall. And then I got licked again when I got home."

"Take me to The Hill," Kenner said. His hand was gripping the handle that hung above the passenger window. The Hill was what we called the old Arkansas State Tuberculosis Sanatorium, closed since the 1970s.

125

I took the winding roads that switch back across the hills and valleys, and the grass was so green it looked painted on. Kenner said, "My Granddaddy Box had the TB. He said when somebody died, the nurses would come by and shut all the patients' doors, but you could hear the gurney, wheels wobbling, rolling down the marble hallways. When the gurney swung back by again, the wheels never shimmied." Kenner looked out the window. "The weight of the body and whatnot," he said. "The weight of what had just happened. I wonder if Granddaddy was thinking of that gurney when he died."

I looked at Kenner then. His mouth was turned down. He rubbed his eyes and breathed hard.

"That place was a masterpiece, though," I said. "The dairy. The rolling hills. The air spiked with honeysuckle in the summer. That main building, five stories plus a basement. It looked like a piece of art."

"I gave Granddaddy cigarettes. It was all I could think to do."

When we got to the edge of the place, Kenner changed his mind. "Bird," he said, "I don't want to go."

I turned the truck around. Kenner's arm still gripped that handle, his skin looking like a land map that speckled with lakes and ponds. It was the blood thinner Kenner took that made his skin look that way.

"I got an idea," I said and leaned hard on the gas pedal. The old truck shook, and then it kicked in, and I got it up to forty miles an hour. Kenner said, "Now you're cooking with propane!" and shifted so that his free hand rested on the dash.

We made it to Kelsey's Bar by two in the afternoon, and there were no other customers there. I got us two beers, and we sat in the corner by the jukebox. I dropped in a quarter and played

"Make the World Go Away" by Eddy Arnold. Kenner closed his eyes and sang along, his voice like something dropped from heaven by mistake.

When the song ended, Kenner sipped his beer. "I forgot how good it was," he said. And I said, "The beer?" (It tasted like flaked soap because of my heart medicine.) And he said, "No, this whole dang planet."

Kenner's hair was white, and he wore it combed back. You could see the comb marks and his pink scalp underneath. He said, "One time I got sunburned so bad my skin was peeling off. That was back when I was framing houses for Goose, and I'd taken my shirt off in the heat. When I got home, Everline cussed me blind and stripped my clothes off and made me get in the tub. The water was lukewarm, but it felt like ice water. She sat on the side of the tub with a A&W root beer mug and she dunked water on my head for a long time. She had a Glen Campbell album going; every once in a while she'd sing along." Kenner looked away. "Happiness stares you in the face when you're young, and you don't even recognize it."

"She must've stole that mug from the A&W," I said, "You couldn't buy one back then."

"You know it!" Kenner said, and he hooked his thumbs in his suspenders like he'd just won something.

After we finished the beers, the bartender asked us if we wanted another. Kenner looked around at the empty tables, the barstools still leaned over like fallen trees at the bar's edge, and he said, "We're going to go drink where there's a little more spirit. This place is drier than Happy Hour at the Betty Ford Clinic."

When we got back in the truck, he said, "Let's go stick our toes in some water."

And so I drove out to Deerbone Creek, to the low-water spot down a rutted road so rough the truck jostled us like cats in a tow sack. A breeze was ruffling the trees, and the sun was warm as a wood stove in winter. We inched down, holding on to each other's shoulder.

We sat on a spot beneath a willow tree that leaned out over the water, easing ourselves down little by little until our butts were safe on the ground. We took off our shoes and then our socks and rolled up our pants. Our legs were shiny white, our feet ugly.

"Mama used to chew the bark of the willow," I said. "It was like aspirin."

"Willows don't live long enough," Kenner said. He looked up. The undersides of the long leaves were white. "But how long is long enough when you think about it?"

I started to answer, but then I realized it was not really a question for me. I felt the leaves, and they were ribbons in my hand. We scooted closer to the creek and stuck our feet in, the cold a jolt through our old bones. The water was green as a 7Up bottle and smelled like fish.

Kenner used my shoulder to push himself up, and he stood in the water, standing on the slippery rocks, lifting his face to the sun. I stood myself, there on the bank, ready to catch him if he started to fall, but he never did. In a minute, he said, "You remember Tank?"

Tank was killed in a car accident when we were all in sixth grade. I said of course I did, and Kenner went on. "He was an Indian, but I don't know if you can say that now. I think you say Native American. Nowadays I mostly keep my mouth shut in public because everything you say can tie somebody's panties in a knot.

"Anyway," Kenner said, "I spent the night at Tank's house one time. His mama made dumplings out of grapes, and they were about as good as anything I'd ever eaten. The next morning, before the sun come up, I saw him from the bedroom window. He was sitting Indian-style on the ground, a few yards away, with his hands raised up above his head. He stayed that way till the sun was up good and proper."

"What was he doing?"

"He was willing the sun to come up. Said he did it every morning. It was one of the best things I ever saw, Bird, and I've been to Talladega to see Bill Elliot race."

"What did you think when Tank died?"

"I thought the sun might never rise again."

"I thought it meant the rest of us could go at any minute, but then I was always thinking about myself," I said, and Kenner said, "You always were too hard on yourself."

You could see tadpoles swimming in packs. Kenner rubbed his arms. I held my right hand out, and he took it, and we walked out of the green water. When he sat back down beneath the willow, I dried his feet with my own socks and put his dark socks back on his feet. I rolled them down—he was the only person I ever knew who rolled his socks that way—and I tugged his shoes back on and tied them.

Inside the truck, with the windows down, you could still hear the creek rushing along. Kenner leaned against the seat and sighed. He had a liver spot by his left eye and a scar that ran across his cheek. I knew the map of his face as well as I did my own. My wife Ocie didn't think men knew how to be friends, and mostly she was right. But somehow me and Kenner had figured it out.

I turned on the radio. That new hopped-up country music was playing, the singer sounding like a beat dog. "What do you want to do now?" I asked Kenner, but he had his eyes closed. I called his name louder, but my friend didn't move an inch, and that's when I understood.

When I think about it now, I figure Kenner was seeing Tank sitting in the clouds, just about then, Tank's hands raised, bringing the sun back to heaven like a boy would do a yo-yo. And then Tank called out the moon, this time just for Kenner, getting it right where it belonged, so even and steady no one on earth would question how this magic worked, even though we'd witnessed it from the day we were born.

Fall

She'll Be Back

She was wearing a blue velvet dress, cut low at the neckline, a slit running up the side of the skirt. Her hair, just barely brown, was in loose curls past her shoulders. What I remember most is that she smelled like carnations and cinnamon gum, and when I slipped the corsage of roses and daisies over her small hand, it wouldn't stay put. She tied it in place, using her teeth to pull the silver ribbons taut against her pale skin.

But it was after the dance, after we'd gotten in trouble for dancing too close—"Couldn't get a piece of notebook paper between you two," Coach Devo had said—that I got to know her. As I drove her home, she pointed down a dark road I wasn't familiar with. "Long cut," she said, her blue eyes shining, and then she slid closer to me, making me go crazy when her thigh touched mine.

There is something about velvet, the way it feels when you touch it. There is something about a dress that comes to a girl's ankles, but then has that one slit that reaches high above her knee. It was too much for me, and in that car, on that night, on that back road that led to the river bottoms and then straight out of Arkansas, I fell in love.

When I look back, I see how our relationship could not have survived. The way we were when we were together made the planet spin too fast, and when I stood next to her, my heart beat irregularly. What I know now is that she was broken in a way I didn't quite understand. She had a father who hit her, I knew that, and a mother who seemed eternally angry. Once, standing on her porch, the clock about to strike midnight, I heard noises coming from inside. Glass shattered, a door slammed, and then the cussing started, her mother's voice recognizable even from a distance. Her face went white when she heard the ruckus. "Mama's at it again," she said. And then, "Go." She turned her face when I tried to kiss her.

All I wanted was to marry her, to make her mine, but I was younger than her by a year and a half, and the guys kept coming around when I wasn't with her. After we'd been together a year, I guess she started to consider what her life would be like without me. In another three months, we were finished.

I can't describe the pain of seeing her go, except to say that even now, all these years later, I have never felt another thing like it. She was stone-faced when she told me it was over. I thought, at first, that she was kidding, but then I looked into her eyes. They were vacant, or maybe worse than vacant. They seemed like eyes that had found the bottom of sorrow and then had dug a little deeper.

"Don't," I said, my voice weak and unconvincing, even to me. She shook her head no, and she tugged at the silver zodiac sign she wore as a pendant, pulling it across the chain there at the base of her fine throat. Her hands were steady; that's what I remember most, while mine trembled so much I shoved them in my pockets.

I sat outside Windsor Park Baptist Church on her wedding day and revved my engine just as "Wedding March" started. I played David Gray's "The One I Love" as loud as I could until her older brother came outside, lit a cigarette, shook his head, and mouthed the word "loser" to me.

A year later, she called me up. "I need to see your face," she said, and we arranged to meet on the railroad tracks near her house at midnight. She had lost weight, not in a good way, and her low-slung jeans looked as if they could fall at any minute. She wore a red silk blouse, and her hair was up in a ponytail. I stood on the tracks and watched her come to me.

We didn't say a word that night. We stood a foot apart and appraised each other. She had her hands in her back pockets; I had my arms crossed. Finally, I reached out and pulled her close enough to kiss her. You can't take another man's wife. That's what I felt, even as I fought desire. I'd been brought up in the church; I understood the sins that guaranteed hellfire and brimstone, and I was still young enough to believe it. Just then, a train whistle howled in the distance, a kind of warning, I'd thought at the time. I took a step back and let her go.

So what do you do when you love somebody the way I loved her? You marry someone else. And I did. I had a good wife, and then I had two good kids, and for a few years, I was happy. If I thought about her, I didn't dwell on it. If she called my house, I never knew. On my wedding day, though, I thought of her. I wanted her outside my church. I wanted her to sit in her car and regret every move she'd made that took her away from me.

I might have stayed married forever, but my wife grew tired

of me. I wasn't a bad husband, but I worked a lot, and when I wasn't working, I hunted whatever was in season. We went to counseling and took tests that indicated I was not "all in" the marriage, and that I had "trouble truly seeing" my wife. While the counselor, who was draped in a pyramid of tie-dyed scarves, said this, I watched my wife. She crossed her right leg over her left knee and swung her foot up and down, and she nodded so hard it looked like her head could snap off. An angry wife, that's what I saw. Who knows what else I was missing.

In my new place, a rickety warehouse with a concrete floor stained by motor oil, my life started feeling like my own again. The kids were teenagers, and they spent about half their time with me. I had a string of women bringing by casseroles, leaving their phone numbers, asking for help lighting their gas fireplaces. On Halloween, the air turned cold, and the wind whistled. I walked outside and leaves skipped across the street. I'd planned to watch *Texas Chainsaw Massacre*, drink a few beers, maybe call the woman who'd dropped off a sack filled with candy corn and popcorn balls.

When she called, I knew her voice instantly. "There's a hole in my heart," she said, and for a minute, I thought she was sick, but she just laughed at me. Twenty minutes later, she was at my door. Her hair was longer than I'd ever seen it, and she had a few lines at the corner of her eyes when she smiled. She was dressed in black: jeans, leather jacket, boots. She wanted to ride.

How she knew I had a motorcycle, I don't know. I'd only gotten the Ducati Monster three weeks before—the first bike I'd had since I was in my twenties. It moved like a sports bike, and I'd been taking it on the back roads, driving faster than I had in years, almost laying it down several times.

When she climbed on behind me, she said, "I like the old-school mirrors," and I laughed.

"That's what you like?" I teased, and she slapped me on the shoulder. She leaned into me as we wound our way through town. When I started showing her what the chopper had on Old Wire Road, she slid her hands beneath my jacket; the feel of them so close was like manna dropping from heaven.

Nothing moves the way a Ducati does, and nothing feels like she did on that night, her chest against my back, her knees pressing into my legs as we rounded bend after bend. I thought for a second that we could keep going, somewhere away from there. When I finally slowed down, she let go of me, held her arms straight out, and rode like that through the darkness.

What I wanted at that moment was to drive off the road and onto the path that led to the forest. I wanted to lift her off that bike and put my arms around her and feel the length of her body against mine. But she was still wearing a wedding ring, and I still wasn't that kind of guy. So I kept driving, and when we got back to my place, I asked, "Why do you stay married to him?"

Her hair was wild from the ride, her eyes bright. She looked ten years younger than she had when she arrived, and I regretted for a moment bringing up the subject.

She shrugged, looked away. "I'm not worth much," she said. I tried to protest, but she raised her hand. "I know you think I am, but I'm not. I don't know how to be with anybody. Not really be," she said. "He doesn't love me, not in any way that matters, so it works out. I leave him alone, he leaves me alone."

"That's no way to live," I said.

"I know," she said. "I know. But I've wrecked every good thing that's come my way—everything except you. You got out just in time," she said, and then she laughed, a shattered laugh that made everything around me feel empty.

I opened two beers, handed her one, then downed mine. She sat in my recliner, the one piece of furniture I'd taken from my house. "I don't remember getting out," I said. "I remember being told to leave."

"All the same," she said, and her mouth turned down. I'd never seen her cry, and I wondered if this was as close as she came.

I poured myself three fingers of whiskey while she stood and walked to the window. I'd yet to put up blinds. "Sorry your marriage didn't work out," she said.

"It worked for a good long while," I said. "It worked well enough."

"My marriage never has worked right. The things I've done—" she said.

"Not my place to judge," I said and took another drink. "Not anybody's place to judge."

She tapped her fingers on the arm of the recliner. It was a habit I remembered well; she had never been able to stay still.

"I had one perfect night in my life," she said. "The night of the dance. Me in velvet, you in that ridiculous tux. I've had a thing for tuxes ever since."

My glass was empty. I could hear a group of kids outside, probably on their way to toilet paper somebody's yard—anything to make Halloween last.

"And I have a thing for velvet, but only if you're in it."

The wind whistled across the roofline. A car drove by with the stereo up. I was treading on treacherous ground. I was sinking into the past.

She stood and handed me her beer bottle. She touched my cheek, and her hand was cold. "I'll try not to come back," she said, and she turned to leave.

"I want you to come back," I said. "Just without the ring."

She didn't even turn around, just shook her head and walked out into the night. Every footfall was a new heartache, but I stood on the porch and watched anyway. And when I finally went inside, I flicked on every light and unlocked the doors. "She'll be back," I said, but of course, there was no one there to hear it.

Rocket Men

The wind was blowing that night, lifting the edges of our skirts, tossing candy wrappers that tumbled end to end across the football field. The field was empty except for the debris, and the scoreboard blinked a row of zeroes in a way that was dizzying if you watched it for too long. There were four of us that night— there were always four of us—and we were wearing knee-high boots and too much eyeliner. Our hair was long and wild as if we'd just climbed out of bed. We could have passed for twenty, though none of us was older than seventeen.

"It feels like the end of something," Kate said, and she pointed to the empty field where forty minutes before our football team, the Alma Airedales, had crushed our biggest rival, the Van Buren Pointers.

"This time next year," I said, "we'll all be somewhere else."

Miller was tapping a spot near her collarbone, a habit she'd had since the day I met her when she'd transferred to Alma in the ninth grade. Her nails were painted burgundy, and she looked like Cleopatra, even in the boots and the white T-shirt with a red satin apple that stretched across the spot where her heart beat. "When we moved here, my dad said we wouldn't stay more than a year." She stopped, her gaze fixed on the visitors' bleachers, although no one was there. "And then Mom left," Miller said. The wind whipped her long hair across her face, and for a moment she was hidden by the darkness of it. "But then I met the three of you." Her voice broke on the word "three," and I felt something tighten in my chest.

Nina stood on one foot. Like a flamingo, I thought. "Let's get out of here," she said. Nina glanced at her watch—it was a guy's watch, and she'd yet to tell us where she'd gotten it, although we'd all asked. "I have to be home by midnight." She shook her head. "Midnight. Can you believe it?"

We cranked up the heat in Miller's car. We were always cold back then, our bodies waif-like from too many diets, too much time spent in front of tall mirrors and fashion magazines. We turned on the radio. Otis Redding came on, and then Neil Young, and then Creedence Clearwater Revival singing a song that asked who would stop the rain. Miller put on another layer of lip gloss, eyed herself in the rearview mirror, frowned.

Her car was old and loud, and Miller drove like she was punishing it. We passed the one cop in town, waved as we flew by, and he flashed his lights but didn't move. On the highway, Miller let it go, and we caught air on the stretch of road that curved back and forth across the dark mountain.

Nina was beside me, and when the headlights of an oncoming car flashed across her face, I stole a look. Her eyes were the green of gemstones. Her hair so black it looked unreal. I watched Miller's hand on the steering wheel. Every finger had a ring. Beside her, Kate sat, the air from the heater moving her hair, lifting it like a red silk scarf caught on a wind current.

"Where are we going?" I asked, and Miller shrugged. Kate reached across the seat, squeezed my knee. "Lake Fort Smith," she said, and then looked at Miller to make sure. "Right?" Kate asked, and Miller nodded.

Clouds hung low in the sky, hiding the moon. When we came to a stop, there was the sound of the spillway rushing below us, thousands of gallons of water screaming across the rocks. When we spoke, our voices barely sounded above the noise.

We grabbed our coats and walked to the cliff where slabs of limestone rock jutted out below in shallow ledges here and there. "Let's climb down," Kate called out, and already she was moving closer, sitting down finally, her tall boots hanging over the edge.

"That's how people die," I said, and I kneeled down beside her. Kate said, "Don't be such a drag."

Miller walked back to the car, started the motor, flicked on the headlights that threw light across all of us. In the glare of the headlights, we could see the water crashing across the rocks. Kate looked at Miller, and then down below. She scooted back to safe ground and spun around so that her back was to the spillway, and I sat down beside her. Nina and Miller stood just feet away.

"I'm not going back to school on Monday," Nina said. She had her arms crossed tight. Her hip jutted out. She looked like a young Elizabeth Taylor standing there, her dark hair billowing, one eyebrow arched just so.

"Of course you are," Miller said, but Nina shook her head no.

"And I'm not going back on Tuesday," Nina said. "Or any other day." On her right hand, she wore her senior ring, the stone icy blue even though our school colors were green and gold. We'd already planned our graduation trip to Gulf Shores. Already had our senior pictures taken. "There's this guy who wants me to leave with him," she said, and I saw her twisting the man's watch on her wrist. It was so loose it could have easily slipped off.

"There's always a guy," I said. "No reason to lose your mind over it."

Kate said, "I get it. If I had a guy waiting, I'd leave this town in the dust." I was so close to her; I could smell the smoke from the wood stove that heated her house and seeped into every outfit she wore after September.

"Who is it?" Miller asked.

"I can't say," Nina said. Miller covered her eyes with her hand and said, "You're breaking my heart."

There was a maple tree that caught the light from Miller's car, and as the wind moved, at least a dozen leaves fell. They were the color of autumn, the color of Kate's hair when the sun hit it. "I'm breaking my own heart," Nina said, "but I can't help it."

Miller lifted her arms like she was directing a choir. "This was supposed to be our year!" Miller's affinity for drama showing in every syllable. "You and me and Kate and Jennie. Our last year. Next year, you can take off with anybody you want, and I won't say a word. I promise."

Kate had taken my hand, and she held it between her own hands, and I could feel her trembling. "We have this moment. This right now. But nothing else. Ask for too much, Miller, and you'll get slapped down! You might as well figure that out now."

Kate's older brother had drowned the year before at Frog Bayou in Rudy. In two years' time, her younger brother would be swallowed up by the Arkansas River after his fishing boat capsized.

"Do you love him?" Miller asked Nina, and Nina laughed. "Of

course not," she said, "but I'm going with him anyway. Mama loves Daddy, and you see how that works out. They fight like ninety percent of the time."

Miller pulled her coat tighter around her. "So you think not loving this guy is going to save you somehow?"

Nina lifted her chin. "I do."

"Then you're an idiot, Nina."

I stepped in then. "Enough, Miller. It's not your life. It's nobody's life but Nina's."

Kate dropped my hand and stood up. "I joined a club," she said, and I pulled away. The four of us didn't join anything. Not choir or band or drama or the yearbook staff. We didn't want our classmates to define us by anything but our friendship with one another. "You did what now?" I asked.

"I joined the Science Club. We meet during sixth period. We think there's life on Mars. We found this photo that looks like there's water there." She stood a little taller. "And we think we can prove it."

Nina got up, brushed off her skirt. It was black like her boots and short, and perfect. "Kate is looking for life on Mars, Miller. Do you think she'll find it?"

"No," Miller said. "I don't. I think Kate's been listening to too much Elton John. All those rocket men." Miller laughed, but the laugh was hollow.

Nina lifted her chin. "Do you think we'll be friends in a year?"

Miller ignored her. "Mom calls sometimes," she said. "Late at night. Early, early morning. I pick up the phone when Dad's not around. She cries a lot. It's not the same as an apology."

"Maybe she didn't know how to stay," Nina said. "Staying is hard."

Miller wiped her eyes. "How far are you going?"

"Tulsa."

"And you'll come back sometimes?"

"Sure I will. After things settle down."

Kate took a step backward, teetered, and for a minute I imagined what it would be like to see her sailing over the edge. I grabbed her wrist and pulled her back and held her close. In five years, Kate would get a diagnosis she couldn't come back from. If I'd known that then, I might never have let her go.

Grabbing Kate, pulling her back, happened in the time it would take you to blink, but it's what I remember most from that night. Not Nina. Nina was the center of the earth, all iron and fire. She would always be fine.

In the car, Miller switched on the radio. Nina looked at her big watch. "It's fifteen minutes till midnight," she said, and Miller sped up. Nina was a girl of contradictions. She couldn't be late for anything, even if she were planning to slip out of her bed later, crawl out the window, step into a brand-new life.

The rain started, soft at first and then furious. At Nina's house, I looked at the mums planted in a circle around the concrete birdbath: rust-colored, orange, purple. Nina said, "I love you all, I really do." And then she stepped out of the car, the hood of her coat pulled up against the rain. When I looked back, she was still standing at her front door under the yellow porch light, her hand raised to us. It was not lost on me that Nina was the one standing still and we were the ones moving away.

On the drive to Kate's house, we didn't talk at all. Above us, Mars sat, as red as an apple, and possibly as wet as the road we were driving. I imagined rivulets of water running down red craters, pooling in red ponds, big-headed green Martians bathing as we drove the back roads of Arkansas. I watched Kate stare out the car's window, this C student I loved, who might one day prove something NASA denied was true. At least she believed in something, I thought. At least she believed.

Where the Tigers Sleep

Twenty-three-year-old Bessie Turner grabs her car keys from the red ceramic bowl that sits on her entryway table she fashioned out of an old wooden ironing board. She runs her hand across its surface, worn smooth by heat and toil.

Outside, this October day is all red leaves and blue skies. So beautiful you'd put it on a postcard if you could.

Bessie left the washing machine running, and as she jumps in the seat of her old Ford Bronco, she hears the rinse cycle start, pushing a whoosh of soapy water from a pipe inside the house straight into her rocky yard.

The rearview mirror needs to be adjusted. Her brother Robbie was the last one to drive the Bronco, and he's a foot taller than Bessie. When he brought it back last night—the gas tank filled for once—he offered her fifteen thousand for it, but Bessie, who could use the cash, didn't consider his offer for a New York minute.

The Bronco is orange with black interior, circa 1977, the year her daddy bought it new when he was just sixteen. She learned to drive in the old monster. This morning she decided to skip work. She looked out her bedroom window, saw the SUV, and decided it needed a drive through the country. As she starts the motor, she imagines her daddy sitting beside her, one arm across the back of the seat, the toe of his work boot raised, as if he were ready to slam the brakes should she need him to.

When he died two years ago, Robbie, who's a year older than Bessie, got the house trailer and the land that went with it. She got the Bronco. She shakes her head, thinking of last night's conversation about her brother's want of the little piece of her daddy she'd been given.

The SUV is loud and rough as it plows through the rutted road that leads to Alma. Bessie likes the way her hands vibrate on the steering wheel when it really gets going.

She's wearing her daddy's favorite belt buckle made of brass and a polished stone that's aqua green with gold flecks. The markings make it look like sand falling through an hourglass. It's one of the few things she took from the house after he died. The buckle, a shoebox of photos, and an old bottle of his pain pills that she keeps in her purse in case some hurt or the other gets to be too much.

Bessie swings the old Bronco onto the two-lane highway that etches through the mountains from Alma to Fayetteville. On her thin wrist, a sling of bangles rattles. She checks her face in the rearview mirror. She has hazel eyes. Black hair. A line that looks like a shot arrow on her forehead. She smiles a half-smile, an act that's supposed to make you feel better even when you don't. She checks the smile, decides it looks ridiculous, digs in her purse for lip gloss and swipes it on.

In the last year of his life, her daddy installed a CD player, rigged it to the Bronco's dash with bailing wire and duct tape, and bought a collection of sad old country songs that could make a teetotaler take to the bottle. Bessie turns it on, and Jim Reeves starts singing "He'll Have to Go."

The song is about a man calling his ex from a pay phone inside a bar, asking her to tell the guy she's with to hit the road.

As the Bronco climbs, the landscape changes. The trees in the hill town of Mountainburg are shaking their heads, scattering red and orange and yellow leaves to the ground. A big yellow dog ambles across the road, a dog who looks like its name should be King or Brando. When she honks, the dog eyes her as if it's thinking, Who died and made you boss?

The school's marching band is practicing on the football field, and Bessie can hear the jaunty notes of what sounds like "Eye of the Tiger."

Her cell phone rings, and she picks it up. "What do you want, Jackson?"

"Just thinking about the other night."

"What about it?" Bessie says, her voice sharp as sewing needles.

"Well, you know, the whole 'seeing other people' talk kind of got off track."

"I think it was exactly on track," Bessie says. "And I think you should see all the other people you want because you won't be seeing me again."

"Now, that's the thing," Jackson says, his voice husky as all get-out. "That doesn't work for me at all."

Bessie passes a sugar maple with leaves as red as a campfire. The mountains smell like earth and pine. Just beside the road is an election sign that reads, "Trust Ted," and she remembers her grandma's warning: Never trust a man who says trust me.

"I don't give a damn what you want," Bessie says, her words a different kind of fire, and ends the call.

Jackson overplayed his hand. He thought he had some kind of hold over Bessie because she never complained. Because she praised every small thing he did for her. What he didn't know is that you can't break a heart that's already broken.

The Bronco still smells like her daddy. Drugstore aftershave that's overblown with menthol and cedar. Cigarette smoke. Pine and oak shavings from the furniture factory where he worked nights for as long as Bessie could remember. One day the smell will go away. The thought feels like an iceberg inside her stomach.

The CD has made its rounds from heartache to heartache and back again. Marty Robbins whined about his mistress, the Devil Woman who caused him to stray. Tammy Wynette advised women to stand by their men. Patsy Cline fell to pieces.

As for Bessie, she drove on, through the Boston Mountains, past Ozark Folkways in Winslow where the hippies had knitted clown-colored sweaters for the old trees out front, had made sleeves for the lowest branches.

When she was a year old, a tornado came through, hit the trailer they were living in at the time, during a freak storm in February. The twister lifted the roof and sucked her out, still in her crib. Bessie's been told she was too young to remember what happened after, but she knows she does. Her daddy stepping over what she now thinks were downed power lines, the glow of his flashlight big as the moon. She can see it still, the round of light catching her eyes, moving up and down the length of the white crib.

Bessie heard her daddy shout, "Thank you, Big Guy!" a statement she thinks was aimed at Jesus. He then called out to a group of other folks who'd been searching. Bessie's crib was stuck in a big oak tree, wedged between two strong limbs. She was barely even wet.

There is a spot a few miles up the road. A piece of land with a white church with a sagging roof and a bell on top. Bessie has loved this place since the beginning of time.

She pulls over, letting the one truck behind her speed by. She skids across the gravel drive and realizes she must have been going faster than she thought. When she parks the car behind the church—she doesn't want anybody stopping to check on her— she pats the Bronco on its hood.

From the back of the SUV, she pulls the old quilt that has more stories than she has time to hear. Whoever takes care of this church has been slacking, and the grass has grown as tall as Bessie's knees. It sways the way grass does, as if dancing, and Bessie opens her hand to touch it.

She lies down on the quilt a few yards away, tugging her leather jacket around her. It is cold today, or at least nearly cold, and a breeze is blowing.

Lying hidden in the tall grass reminds her of childhood. She'd take this very quilt and find a spot in the hay pasture where her daddy had planted alfalfa. Nobody thought he could grow it in Arkansas, but he was tired of bermudagrass, and he'd gotten some advice from the guy at the Agriculture Extension Service.

He was smarter than anyone knew.

She loves the way the tall grass makes a cushion beneath the quilt that is gray and yellow and white. The sun is nearly directly above her, and she keeps her sunglasses on against it.

For months now, Bessie has tried to move on. Two years is a long time to grieve, but she feels like she's somewhat of an expert on how to do it. Jackson was an attempt to push forward, but Jackson was a player. Before him, she'd spent too much money on her only credit card. When she thinks how long it's going to take to pay it off, her whole body tenses.

From inside the church, she can hear a piano playing, a woman singing. She raises up on her elbow, feeling like someone who's been caught, but then she decides she's not doing anything wrong anyway.

The song is "I Saw the Light," and the woman singing has the voice of the mountains. You can smell woodsmoke in her words. You can hear bacon frying on a Sunday morning.

Bessie puts her head back down and goes still. Clouds tumble across the sun, and she lies in shadow. She wonders what it's like to have faith that doesn't short-circuit the way hers does. She prayed so hard for her daddy. She got on her knees that one time, right beside his hospital bed.

The world without her daddy is like a jungle at night. Bessie doesn't know what her feet are touching. She doesn't know where the tigers sleep.

The woman in the church is singing about the absence of sorrow, about blindness, grief. She sings like she's made peace with sorrow.

What faith did her daddy have? He believed there would always be work for the willing. He believed a three-legged dog was a sign of luck. He believed his soul would live on after the grave.

Bessie hasn't prayed once since her daddy died. If the whole world falls down, let it fall. She thinks about a poem she read in high school that had this line: The avocado on the windowsill is a benediction. The old woman with her hands folded, waiting for nothing is a prayer.

She thought the poem was filled with errors, but now she's not so sure. Maybe her hand on the Bronco is a spiritual thing, the sweatered trees in Winslow, the yellow dog sure that he'll make it across a trafficked road. Bessie says aloud, "Amen and amen."

The woman in the church continues to sing.

As Long as You Remember

He came up from Texas, in a Dodge Ram that blew a gasket on the outskirts of Big Town, and that stalled him for a time, but still he came. It didn't matter that the Dodge was not his, that it belonged to a blonde he met in a dive called Cactus Jack's, where the drinks were watered down, and the jukebox played nothing but Waylon. The blonde, sitting on his lap by then, was near about passed out when he fished her jangly keys out of her jacket pocket and planned his getaway. "Give Chick a little sugar, Sugar," he said, and she turned her face to him, and her eyes looked right into his soul, which at that moment was a waxy thing, he said, something a flame could whittle down to nothing.

The cab of the truck was a mess, filled with McDonald's cups and beer cans and trash sacks of dirty laundry. A dream catcher swung from the rearview mirror, fast as a schoolyard swing, when Chick tore out of the parking lot. There was a picture of a cotton-topped boy glued to the dash, no more than three, Chick said, and an ID badge in the ashtray from the casino where the blonde worked.

Sorrow is what he felt in that truck, but still, he kept going. Sorrow, Chick said, was everywhere, in the pearl-colored moon, in the spiky arguments rattling the windows of the houses he passed on the way out of town, in the bellyaching of the ambulance that caused him to pull the Dodge off the road as it passed, its lights blood red on that navy blue night.

That's why he kept singing like he did, to ward off the sorrow. Mostly, he sang Johnny Cash songs, he said, the sorrow and the stolen truck with the picture of the boy were the things that seemed to push in on him, that seemed loud as hornets on stretch after stretch of highway. He didn't travel the interstate. He didn't trust big roads with big signs that made big promises about motels that felt like home, or diners with meals like your mama made, or churches where the good Lord welcomed you no matter how junky you dressed, no matter if you didn't have the good manners to bow your head when the Invitation started.

How he got to Louisiana, he couldn't quite say. It wasn't how he intended to go. What he intended was a straight shot, crossing over in Texarkana, cutting through the guts of Arkansas, and ending up at Good Samaritan Hospital, where I was. It could have been the singing, Chick said, because Johnny made him cry, even "A Boy Named Sue," which most folks took as a jokey song, even though it cut like a chainsaw when you thought about it. A drunk, mean daddy who cuts off part of his son's ear, and still the boy loves the old cuss, deep down he loves him, which is an abomination when you come right down to it, the way the daddy acts, the way the boy aches, all that hurt leaving scars wider than any two-lane highway.

In Shreveport, the Dodge with the dirty clothes caught fire while Chick slept nearby on a park bench at a roadside rest stop.

He woke to see it, the flames orange and blue and jumping, the windshield booming apart, glass everywhere, he said.

He walked after that, straight down the road, his belly empty as a cave, his thumb stuck out. He had two dollars then, and sixty-six cents, and a picture of me, and my phone number written in red on the corner of a Valentine I'd got him once, all inside the wallet he made in Leatherworks when he was in county lockup six months back.

The second guy who picked him up, Chick said, was a squatty businessman who had an answer for everything, even when there wasn't no questions asked. "There is nothing new under the sun," he said to Chick when they passed a subdivision going up, trees getting knocked down, men scrambling up scaffolding to lay down bricks on new houses that would all look the same, cement trucks churning out concrete, like giant ants with the stomach flu.

"I come alive," Chick said, "brand-new. Every morning," and the guy seemed to puzzle the thought, stroked his chin where a pink scar cut across just under his bottom lip, and then he adjusted the rearview mirror on the Buick.

"But every day you're older," the guy finally said, "And every day you fall into your old, hard ways," and then he switched on the radio to an Oldies station that played Steppenwolf like it was 1972. "And I must say, I feel like I've known you, or someone like you, in my past, and that we've had this exact conversation before."

"I get that a lot," Chick said, not because it was true but because it hurt his head to talk to people who didn't know how to live. Outside, Chick said, the grass waved along the highway. Red clover stood amidst it. black-eyed Susans, long-legged, yellow as a kid's rain slicker, seemed to rock along with the radio, and all this guy could see was yesterday's news.

Chick got dropped off in Donette and worked for four days hoeing soybeans. The plants tangled low to the ground, and as he walked through the sharp vines cut at his bare legs, since he'd taken to working in his T-shirt and boxers. If he wore his jeans, he said, the morning dew soaked him through, kept him soggy until the sweat started and then he was damp all over again.

He cut out as soon as he got paid, five twenty-dollar bills, four ones, seven pennies. He'd eaten with the other workers, he'd slept in a row house on an army cot, and it wasn't bad, he said, if you didn't mind the snoring, if you didn't mind the lies the young guys told about the girls they had in town.

Chick swiped the foreman's ride, an El Camino, half truck, half car, turquoise blue, and rode through the river bottoms late that night, the windows down. The sorrow he'd felt earlier was waning then, and the moon was blameless that night, big and round and fuzzy at the edges. He loved the river bottoms. He loved the irrigation systems that looked like giant metallic caterpillars, arching up and inching down, and they shone like starlight every time the moonlight hit them. He switched the radio on, and Dolly was singing, and he could see her if he closed his eyes, which he did on the straightaway, her yellow hair curling, her red lips smiling.

He left the El Camino two towns over, just as morning broke. The foreman had been kind, he said, and the car was spotless when he took it, so it didn't seem right to snatch it clean away. He bought a bus ticket to bring him home, and he settled in next to a round old woman who chanted the names of all her dead relatives as she rocked back and forth. "They are not dead as long as you remember," she said when he asked her why.

A chill ran through him, Chick said. He knew something different. He knew, right then and there, if he spilled my name, I would cross the Thin Place between here and the Great Beyond without so much as a Fare Thee Well. He spied another seat, he said, right up front where he hated to sit, but he took it anyway, just to get away. He started to relax, and then this happened: Chick almost said my name—Sylvia. He opened his lips, and the sound started, his tongue jumping to the back of his bottom teeth. He closed his mouth tight against it. The next thing he did was shut his eyes, rest his elbows on his knees and press his thumbs into his forehead. When he opened them again, the sky had dropped the way it does when the clouds roll in. Dirt from the cotton fields was blowing up, swirling like a magic spell, he said, hanging above the thorny plants.

He didn't eat the last day on the bus, he said. He drank Pepsi Colas, and he chewed gum, and in the bathroom, he raked a bum razor across his whiskers, and when he sat back down, he swallowed my name again and again. When the Greyhound pulled into the station, he jumped, missing the bus steps altogether, and he took off for Good Samaritan.

It was ten blocks away, and Chick was running fast as he could, his work boots slapping the city streets, his button-up shirt wadded up and clutched in his right hand, the wind blowing through his sandy hair, cars honking as he plowed through rush hour traffic. Folks shouted, but he couldn't hear right, so all the yelling blended into everything else until he felt like he was inside a beehive, and all the sounds were wings flapping to keep something alive.

There is a trick light plays inside a hospital. Night could be day or day could be night. You look at the window, and the sky is always the same: gunmetal gray, even at midnight, even at noon. It's hard to walk steady under light like that, and so I quit walking, and then I quit sitting up, and then I just quit.

Chick was racing along the sidewalks, his big arms pumping, his legs stretching farther and farther out as he got nearer and nearer to me. He was reciting the names of those who'd crossed over: his Grandmama Beverly; his second-grade teacher, Miss Jones; his old dog, Ratchet; his brother, Titus; and on and on until even his first parole officer got named.

Pictures of them were rolling through my mind as he named the dead. I did not mind the images, not until he said, "Sylvia, Sylvia, Sylvia," the same way he'd said it on the night we met, urgent, as if he was trying to ground me to him. "Sylvia, Sylvia, Sylvia," he said on that first night when I was still a beautiful woman, and we stayed up until all hours, watching the sun set together, watching it rise again. We lay in each other's arms in those first fresh days and kept every bit of bother away.

There on the sidewalk, he stopped when he chorused my name, bent over with his hands on his knees, gulping air like a dying trout. He let the tears fall, and they made muddy roads down his dusty face. Across his leathery neck. "What have I done?" he said to the ground.

I clutched the hospital bed's scratchy blanket, orange colored and terrible. Held it tight as I could as I watched the ceiling open. I called out, "We kept this ruination away for longer than most people do, Chick, we surely did." I took a ragged breath before I said the last of it, the last of everything that was to come. "You and me kept it away for longer than I ever thought possible."

Mama Says She Loves Me, but She Lies

"My mama says she loves me, but she lies," Wesley Kidd, near about thirty years old, calls out to anybody that'll listen. He's standing in the middle of Talawanda Street, right where it crosses Main, and two cars are stopped now, waiting him out. This is a small place, and if you're downtown on a Tuesday like this particular one, at one-thirty in the afternoon, you probably ain't got nowhere else to be.

Wesley's mama is sitting on the one bench we got, a few feet away, there by the stop sign. Wesley has caused her trouble before; Wesley don't think like a full-fledged grown person. His mama sits with her flowerdy cotton dress pulled down tight across her knees, a ratty sweater slung across her shoulders. Her back is straight like a flagpole, her hands in fists in her lap. She watches Wesley with her pale blue eyes as he paces back and forth across Talawanda.

"Come on now, Wes," his mama says. "You know that ain't

true."

"You lie so much the truth looks the other way when it sees you coming," Wesley says.

"Get on out of the street, Honey," his mama says. "Let these good people pass."

Wesley shakes his head no, and his blond hair falls across his eyes. He bends over, puts his hands on the knees of his overalls. "Mama says she loves me," he says again. "Lies."

"What part is a lie, Wes?" his mama asks.

Old Mr. McKinnon in the yellow Ford truck has been listening through his open window. He cuts off his ignition. He gets out, puts his hand across his shiny forehead, like a salute, to shield his eyes, says, "Wesley, son, I would give a truckload of dollar bills to have one more minute with my dearly departed mama."

Wesley stops his pacing, says, "Did she love you?"

"Oh, my, how she loved me," Mr. McKinnon says, and then he knuckles under the weight of that sentence and has to wipe his eyes.

"Might she have lied about it?" Wesley asks.

"Not a chance," Mr. McKinnon says.

Wesley points to the bench where his mama is thumping one foot against the grass like a guilty person. His mouth is turned down, and he drops his fist to rub his eyes, and he is clumsy when he does it. "That one lies when the truth stands beside her yelling, 'Boo!'"

Bessie Thorton is in the car behind Mr. McKinnon. She hits reverse, puts her arm up on the seatback, and scoots down the road until she can swing it around and head away from here. She has a husband who expects his dinner on the table by four. She has obligations.

Wesley's mama waves at Bessie as she retreats. She gets up off the bench, using the arm of the thing to help hoist her up. At forty-seven, she's not an old woman, but she looks like one, her hair already mostly gray, and when she stands, she is stooped, her shoulders pulling in toward the earth.

"Seems like we've run off Mrs. Thorton," she says.

"Never you mind," Mr. McKinnon says. "She wouldn't want you to worry about her when you have your own trouble." And when he says this, he points to Wesley, who points right back.

Wesley has found three smooth stones, and he is pitching them toward the streetlight, pinging the wire cage that protects the light bulb.

"Sugar," his mama says. "What have I told you about throwing rocks?"

Wesley has another stone in his hand, and he lets it fall to the street. "I could hurt somebody," he says.

"You could hurt somebody," Wesley's mama says.

Mr. McKinnon speaks up. "My mama and I had a falling out. She didn't like Maren, my wife. She had seen Maren outside the Majestic Theater with a gentleman who seemed quite interested in her. When I confronted her, Maren said it was just our insurance agent from two towns over, discussing our coverage, and I chose to believe her. And so I quit talking to my mama, for three years, and when they told me she was in the hospital, I didn't go for two whole days."

Wesley is swatting a fly that is buzzing his right ear. "I don't like that story," Wesley says, and he begins to rock on his big feet, the laces of his work boots undone and hanging loose.

Wesley's mama is standing on the curb now. In two steps she

161

could touch her boy, but she stays put.

"I've never told a living soul that story," Mr. McKinnon says. "I have wanted to, over the years, especially after Maren left me. In the end, she said she hated the ground I walked on." Mr. McKinnon laughs, a sharp, unhappy laugh. "My mama was right about her. Not up to snuff, after all."

A dog howls, and Wesley says, "Your wife didn't love you. She lied."

Mr. McKinnon says, "A wife's love is not like a mama's love. It can go cold as soup left on the kitchen table on a January night over the least little thing. Or your wife can love you like Christmas when she first meets you and then forgets what all the fuss was about before the next spring comes. But a mama, now that's a horse of a different color. Your own mama," he begins, but Wesley puts his hands over his ears and starts to hum.

"What's gotten into him?" Mr. McKinnon says to Wesley's mama.

Wesley's mama tugs a hanky from her dress pocket, twists it into a small rope. "He heard me talking on the telephone," she says. "I was talking to my sister, Levita, and I was saying how I always dreamed of going to Maine and eating a lobster the size of a housecat, and then I said the next wrong thing, that I truly regret, Mr. McKinnon, I do. I said, 'But all my traveling days ended when Wesley was born. All my days from then on out were set in stone.' And then Levita asked me why I wouldn't go ahead and put Wesley in a home, and I told her I thought about it sometimes, like I thought about taking a long, bubble bath, but I couldn't do it as long as I had strength enough to carry him along. When she pushed me, I said, 'I'd be lying if I said it was easy. I'd be a hypocrite if I said I didn't think about another life, with

Wesley altogether whole and living on his own, and happy, and me getting on with the little bit that's left of life.'"

Wesley picks up a stick that's fallen in the road. He whips the air with it, says, "See there! Mama hates my guts!"

"The tongue of man," Mr. McKinnon says, "is as an untrained dog."

The A&M train rumbles by on the tracks three blocks over, shouting with its whistle. When it stops, Mr. McKinnon says, "My own mama was too far gone when I got to the hospital. She was breathing with a rattle. She had gotten so old in the time I'd neglected her. I have not recovered from it, not in all these years."

I have never seen a grown man cry until now, and it is worse than the screechy sirens on the one ambulance we got here in Lurton.

"When I went to clean out her house, she still had pictures of me hanging on the wall, and one by her bedside table," Mr. McKinnon says. "That's how a mama loves, Wesley."

A dump truck rumbles up, and the driver sees Wesley in the road and calls out, "Y'all got trouble?" And Mr. McKinnon sniffs, wipes his wet eyes, says, "Just the normal amount, sir. And we're figuring it out as we speak." The driver honks his horn twice, waves, then backs up and takes Ridge Road out of here.

Wesley's mama says, "I give up, Wesley, I really do. I can't think of another thing to say. Maybe you should go live with Mr. McKinnon. Maybe you'd be happier without your old ma."

Mr. McKinnon stops his crying on a dime, says, "Now, now. No need for drastic measures. I have found that a good meal, a little rest, fixes just about everything." He scratches his head, walks up to Wesley, who lets him put his arm around his shoulder.

"No," Wesley's mama says. "I am not fit, I don't believe. Wesley's right to be mad at me. And I've lied a lot in my life. Every day, practically. I tell Thomas down at Humpo's Quick Stop that I am fine when I'm not fine. I tell the Good Lord I'm grateful when I truly am not. I tell Wesley we're living on Easy Street when mostly I don't know how we're going to get through the next week."

Wesley seems to consider this. He tugs at his ear, then says in a voice that breaks my heart, "But do you lie when you say you love me?"

Well, Wesley's mama comes undone at this. I think for a minute her knees might buckle. Wesley must think so too because he runs to his mama, pats her hair, then takes her hand. When she recovers her wits, she says, "I have never once lied about that, Baby Doll, not one time in my long, sorry life."

Sheriff Comstock, a squat man with dentures, has gotten wind of the trouble on Talawanda Street and heads this way. He does not like confrontation, which is a problem for a lawman. But before he gets all the way up here, Mr. McKinnon calls out, says, "We're all right, Sheriff. Just had a bit of a philosophical conversation going, trying to find the root of a mother's love. Trying to find the depth of it."

And then Wesley straightens his shoulders and says, "Mr. McKinnon and me was about to take Mama over to the Shiloh Cafe, see if she could find her a big ole lobster, a big ole red bug of a lobster because my mama always wanted one of them things, and sometimes you got to get your mama what she wants because life is not easy for mamas, even when you think it is"

"Well, go on, then," the sheriff says, his hands on his wide hips. "Go eat some lobster and let this town get back to its business."

Wesley's mama nods to the sheriff, and then she turns her attention to Mr. McKinnon. "Oh, Mr. McKinnon," she says, "Wesley was just joking. We'll go on home now." But then Mr. McKinnon says, "All this talk of lobster has made me a bit peckish myself. And I could do with a little company, and I'd love to buy y'all some supper." Mr. McKinnon smiles then, the first time I recall seeing him smile in years, and then he opens the passenger door on the cab of his truck and sweeps his other hand real theatrical like. And Wesley and his mama climb in, thinking their own thoughts, maybe thinking a good meal, a little rest, will fix every hurt thing that ever happened. It's not likely to be so, but who has the heart to tell them that?

Landslide

Layla has been making Thanksgiving dinner since she was in her late teens. The first time was the year her mother died. The death had taken place in March, on a day so windy the newly blossomed trees shook like windsocks at a car dealership, and Layla's wrap dress blew open on her walk into the hospital for the very last time.

She thinks of it now, shudders. She'd rambled on once she'd gotten to her mother's room at nearly noon, about the wind, the price of gasoline, the gossip she'd heard at the beauty salon the last time she was there. She hadn't slept much the night before, and she was a little hungover besides. When she looked up, she saw her dad holding her mother's limp hand and the preacher holding his Bible, sitting in the only chair in the room. The lights were out, the beeping machines turned off. How could she have missed all that?

Layla hadn't cried, not then, not for a long time after. The world seemed as empty as the Tundra, and her eyes felt dry. In the elevator that stopped at the parking garage, an older woman told Layla what lovely skin she had, and Layla smiled weakly. It seemed to take all the energy she had.

Her dad told her, in the days that followed, he'd often end up at the hospital, his car with a mind of its own. "The old Camaro is like a lost dog looking for home," he'd said, and then his voice caught.

That first year, Layla had made place cards, had carefully written out her guests' names. She'd ordered flowers—daisies and carnations—that came in a real pumpkin, carved into a vase. She'd bought a cotton tablecloth and matching napkins.

Before everyone sat down properly, her dad rolled the TV into the dining room and turned on a college football game. Layla slipped outside to pull herself together.

She's gotten Thanksgiving down to a science now. Paper plates, canned drinks cooling in the washing machine she fills with ice, a stack of plastic containers ready for leftovers she parses out to her guests. She still uses her mother's recipes, and every Thanksgiving morning, she feels her mother with her, feels the blessing of her childhood when she woke to a house smelling like cornbread dressing, yeast rolls, cherry pie.

On those distant mornings, her mother's fruit salad, made the night before, waited in the refrigerator. It was pink from the juice of the maraschino cherries. It was bolstered by the sour cream and whipping cream, the miniature marshmallows, the cans of Mandarin orange slices and pineapple chunks. The pecans came from trees you could see from their kitchen window. Until Layla moved away, she'd never considered those pecan trees at all, and now she sees what a gift they were, towering above everything, dropping their nuts in rough green pods that stained your fingers when you pried them open.

Layla makes the fruit salad every year, even though none of her three kids will touch it. Her daughter Abigail, sixteen years old and filled with enough anger to start a war, asked just last week, "What part of that slop is a salad?" and Layla felt the blood rise to her face. Layla is seeing a therapist now, and she turned to her cellphone and jotted down this question for the next session, "Are mothers allowed to dislike their own children?"

Her two sons, Evan and Abe, twelve and fourteen, are opposed to the pinkness of the salad, the thing Layla loves the most, although when they were younger, it didn't bother them at all.

In two days, her dad will show up with his wife, Louise. They've been together nine years now, and still it shocks Layla to see the woman, the shiny wedding ring on her finger, the way she leans against Layla's dad's shoulder when they sit on the couch. Louise seems like an interloper, a placeholder, the credits that roll after a movie when almost everyone is walking out of the theater. Louise won't touch the salad either.

The day before Thanksgiving, Layla is making the fruit salad. She forgot to divide her mother's recipe and realizes how much of it will go to waste. Layla's husband, Will, walks through the kitchen, glances up, and says, "Why'd you make all that?"

Layla feels the burn in her nose, the closing of her throat, the fire in her eyes. The precursors to a flood of tears, if she's not careful. If she says what she's thinking right now, she could start a blaze that might take down her whole marriage, so instead, she says, "Dad wanted me to make enough for him to take home."

It's a lie, but lately, most everything Layla says is a lie. You get to be middle-aged, life doesn't turn out, and you start to distort the truth. Just last Saturday, she told the checker at the market that she works out five days a week. The girl looked at Layla's waistline, crossed her arms, and said, "Which gym?" and Layla hauled her jiggly butt out of there.

When her dad arrives on Thanksgiving, he's carrying two pies from a café where he eats breakfast most mornings. Louise doesn't cook much, another thing Layla doesn't approve of. He kisses Layla on the forehead, and she sighs so loud she startles herself.

"Anything wrong?" he asks, and she shakes her head no. Another lie.

"Where's Will?" he asks, and she points to the patio door, where she can see her husband holding his phone to his ear, his other hand in his pocket. He's rocking on his feet, a habit Will's had for as long as she's known him.

Her dad says, "He looks busy. I'll not bother him."

Layla supposes she shouldn't resent her husband for not helping. She supposes she shouldn't resent her father for calling her husband "busy" when she is the only one busy in this house. She pushes a damp lock of hair off her forehead and checks the oven where the dressing is baking, nearly perfectly golden.

At the dinner table, Layla's dad says grace. His voice is smaller than it used to be, and she opens her eyes to watch him pray.

Platters and bowls go around the table. Layla is as good a cook as her mother was, although she'll never own up to it. Midway through the meal, she remembers the fruit salad in the refrigerator. This year she used the extra cherries to make a happy "L" on the surface, a tribute to her own name.

Her daughter Abigail shakes her head when Layla sets the salad on the table, and Layla watches her daughter's smirk that threatens to unravel her. "Some people actually LIKE this dish!"

Layla says, her shoulders shaking, and Abigail says, "I'd like to see a show of hands on that."

Evan and Abe laugh, but then they take a second look at their mom and snap their mouths shut.

Will asks, "What's the 'L' for?" and Layla's dad answers, "Why, my sweet Louise, of course."

For a second or two, Layla doesn't recognize her own laughter. It is too high-pitched, too hysterical to belong to her, but there it is. She squares her shoulders. "Actually, it's for Layla, Dad." She jabs herself in the chest with her thumb. "For me. A thank-you for keeping tradition alive."

Layla is weeping now, and Abigail is sitting up straight. Louise seems especially interested in her napkin, and her cheeks bloom red. Layla sweeps her hand through the air. "All of this, Mom's dressing, her rolls, the salad, I do it to keep her with us." Layla touches the spot on her chest just above her heart. "I do it to keep her *here*."

Layla's therapist calls her mother's death *The Big Trauma*. It short-wired something inside Layla, caused her to become a cautious, suspicious, precise person.

A year after her mother got sick, Layla began to behave badly. As her mother grew weaker, Layla decided God was mad at her, and was showing it by letting her mother waste away. Even though she believed she held her mother's life in her hands, she couldn't stop what she was doing. The worst of it was a guy named Rennie, four years older, smooth-talking, sly. She was with him in the apartment he shared with four roommates the morning her mother died and the entire night before. Layla knows that if she'd stayed home, she'd have been there for the last moments of her mother's life. She could have said goodbye.

The worst part was that she didn't break up with Rennie. He dropped her two months later, saying he'd waited as long as he could for Layla to "get over it."

She has yet to tell this part of her story to the therapist, or to anybody else for that matter. She feels as if saying this out loud will open a river inside her, and that the river will roar out, taking everything down with it. Now, though, she realizes staying quiet doesn't stop a thing. The landslide she's fought so hard against has already begun.

She makes a sound like a hurt animal, then holds her hand tight over her mouth to stop it.

Abigail nearly jumps out of her chair. She shakes her head as if trying to clear her thoughts, then takes the crystal bowl and scoops out a spoonful of fruit salad. She passes the bowl to Evan and Abe, who each take helpings. Will is next. His plate is half-full of the stuff when he's finished dishing it out. Louise takes a helping, the pink fluff bright against the white plate, and then dumps even more onto Layla's dad's plate.

"Stop me if I've told this story before," Louise says, "but I was only twelve when my mother died. Mama loved buttermilk with cornbread crumbled up in it. She'd eat it for supper on scorching summer days."

The boys groan, and Louise wrinkles her nose at them. "I know," she says. "I hated the stuff myself, but in the months after her death, I craved it. I eat it sometimes still, when I'm feeling considerably lonely. I still don't like it, but I *need* it."

Layla's dad clears his throat. "Your mama cut that recipe out of the Courier newspaper one year." Layla's dad pronounces it "Core-your." "It was all the rage with ladies' groups. She thought it was mighty cosmopolitan. That's the word she used,

cosmopolitan. When she served it that first year, I went on and
on about it." He clears his throat again. "I loved making your
mama happy."

Layla remembers that Thanksgiving. She'd still been a kid.
Nothing earth-shattering had happened to her yet. Her biggest
worry was whether she'd ever have a boyfriend, if she'd ever be
as pretty as her mom. Boyfriends came soon enough, but she'd
never be the beauty her mother was.

Will pulls out Layla's chair, pats the seat of it. "Sit," he says,
and when she does, he rubs her back and says, "Great dinner,
babe." While Layla wishes he'd say something more profound,
she appreciates this small effort.

Abigail says, "Hey, Grandpa, tell us what Mom was like when
she was a kid. Did she ever ditch school or sneak out at night?"
and Layla's dad gives his daughter a sideways glance, "Glory be,
did she ever!"

Evan and Abe laugh. Layla holds her breath. Surely he won't
tell the stories that could break her in two.

Layla's dad winks at his daughter, and she feels her shoulders
relax. This will be an easy story, one that puts her in a better light
than she deserves.

Just then, Louise takes Layla's hand and holds it. The light
through the dining room windows is like spun gold. Louise smells
like gardenias and roses. Her hand is bigger than Layla's and soft
as moonbeams. Layla barely registers her dad's voice as he tells
his story. Instead she's thinking about a news report she saw
recently. An entire hillside was taken down by rain, by erosion,
by man's mishandling of what God gave them. She squeezes her
stepmother's hand. But later, the grass came back, and saplings
sprouted, and in valleys, a million swaying flowers bloomed.

Miss Maizie County's Public Disgrace

It all started because Mama was caught standing buck naked in the picture window of her living room. The sheriff came out and talked to me about it. If Mama had lived in the country, it wouldn't have been much of a problem. But she lived in town, and that's a whole different thing. Plus, her house sat across from Bethel Baptist Church. Apparently, the Sunday morning crowd had gotten an up-close-and-personal look at Mama. Even hellfire and brimstone can't compete with a naked woman standing atop a divan, kind of spread-eagle and pressed up against a plate glass window.

Mama's little display didn't come as any great surprise to me. She'd always been a little peculiar, and ever since Daddy died, she'd been on a slow decline. Daddy took care of her, though. Had his life insurance doled out to her in monthly payments so she wouldn't spend it all at once and be left penniless.

After the sheriff's visit, I came on into town and loaded Mama up. Brought her back home with me, fixed up the spare bedroom for her. Now granted, she had days when she was just as right as rain. But there were times when she wandered off. And after I found her wading with the cattle in the neighbor's pond, I knew it was more than I could handle. Doc Patton checked her out, put his hand on my shoulder, and announced she'd gone senile. Advised me to take her over to the Haven O' Rest nursing home. Which I did. There wasn't any way I could look after her full-time, and she'd gotten to the point where she had to be watched.

The story should have ended right there, with Mama in the rest home, me alone in my trailer house on Red Dog Road, and Brother Debo preaching to a crowd of church folks whose image of my naked mother was fading week by week.

But then he came by, Brother Debo did, on a Thursday afternoon. It was my day off from that over-priced diner where I work. Some uppity little debutante from Georgia moved to town with her lawyer husband and opened it last fall. Named it "Garden of Eating," if you can believe that. I waitress there six days a week.

I opened the door to Brother Debo, who was dressed in a black polyester suit and tie. It must have been ninety-five degrees outside, and there he was dressed like he was about to preach a funeral.

"Miss Huggins," he said, "I don't believe you know me. I'm Ransom Debo, pastor of Bethel Baptist Church. I was wondering if I might have a little talk with you."

Once he came inside, I swept the magazines off the divan and motioned for him to sit down. "Florene," I said. "My name's Florene. I prefer that to Miss Huggins if you don't mind."

I sat in the rocking chair facing him, one leg tucked

underneath me. "Just what can I help you with?"

He reached across the coffee table and took my hand. "I know you've had some hard times with your mother," he said. "Doc Patton mentioned you had to put her away in the rest home. I'm sure sorry to hear that. I didn't know your mother well, but she did visit me a time or two at the church office. I recall she brought me strawberry jam and a few tomatoes from her garden once."

I waved my free hand in his direction. "Wait a minute, Preacher," I said. "Don't go acting like you have any kind of affection for my mama. It seems to me if that was the case, you wouldn't have sicced the law on her the way you done. The sheriff said you were dang near hysterical when you called to complain."

Brother Debo let loose of my hand and fiddled with his tie tack. It was a little gold Bible with a ruby where the "O" in Holy should have been. I looked right at him. He wasn't much older than me. Maybe thirty-one or thirty-two. And handsome. Even in that preacher get-up, he was handsome.

In a minute he looked down, pulled a hanky out of his suit pocket, and wiped his brow. "Let's start over Miss Huggins... I mean Florene. There's not a reason in the world we can't be civil to one other. I truly am concerned about your mother." He cleared his throat. "However, there is another reason I'm here."

Big surprise, I thought, and almost said so, but he just kept on talking.

"You see, Florene, since your mother's house is directly across from the church sanctuary, it would make a perfect addition to Bethel Baptist. If I do say so myself, since I took over as pastor, attendance has been soaring. In fact, we're running out of Sunday school space. If we had your mother's house, we could move all the adult classes out there and add a nursery in the main building."

I remember looking into his eyes. They were green with gray rims around the pupils. Kind of like cat eyes.

"Well," I said. "I'll consider it. But don't think just because you're a preacher I'll be giving Mama's house away."

Brother Debo stroked a throw pillow on the divan like it was a lap dog. He smiled at me. He had a little chip in his front tooth and a gold cap farther back on one of his molars. "I find prayer helpful when I have an important decision to make," he said.

"Pray all you want to, Preacher," I said. "I believe I'll do some digging, see what property is going for in Mama's neighborhood."

After he had left, his place there on the divan smelled of musky aftershave and spearmint gum. When I sat down where he had been, the cushions were still warm. I ran through our conversation in my head. The thought of him made my face burn. It was funny I felt that way. I usually couldn't stand preachers.

The following Thursday I woke up early, curled my hair, painted my fingernails. I can't say I was expecting Brother Debo, but I sure was happy when I saw his powder-blue Lincoln inching down my road.

"Florene," he said when I answered the door. "Just stopped by to see if you've decided anything." He shifted his weight from one foot to the other. "I just thought…" He stopped then, ran his fingers through his hair. He was towering above me, shading me from the rest of the world.

I noticed he'd traded in his preacher garb for jeans and a starched white shirt. "Lord," I said, "where are my manners?" I turned and headed for the kitchen. "I made some lemonade if you're interested."

I poured the lemonade into two cut-glass goblets I'd gotten inside boxes of Quaker Oatmeal. After a while, the conversation turned to marriage. All at once he didn't sound like a preacher. Even the way he talked changed. He sounded kind of regular, like somebody you'd meet at the Piggly Wiggly on Double Coupon Night.

Brother Debo sat across from me and moved his glass in little circular motions. "You ever been married, Florene?" he asked.

"Ain't something I generally talk about," I said. "But yeah, I've been married. I was eighteen years old. I'd just been crowned Miss Maizie County for the third time. Did you know, Brother Debo, that I was Miss Maizie County three years running? Ain't nobody beat my record, not in all these years. They have my name etched in the sidewalk down at the high school. Ever so often I go down there, just so I can walk across my own name.

"Anyway, Jess Harrell Nycutt was one of the judges for that last contest. His daddy owned the feed store. I figured he had ambition, what with his family owning a business and all. Course Mama warned me not to marry him, said he wasn't nothing but a pretty boy. But then I never was one to listen to her."

I wiped the sweat beads off the lemonade glass with my thumb. "We'd been married less than a year when Jess's daddy fired him. Jess had been stealing from the cash drawer.

"We moved over to Crossett. Jess thought there'd be more career opportunities. Turned out he was right. Within a month, I was holding down two jobs. Funny thing was, Jess was still looking for employment. He told me he couldn't take any old position, what with his two full semesters of junior college to consider.

177

"Well, after a while he took to drinking and running around, I'm pretty sure. I never had proof, but a girl knows."

Brother Debo took my hand for the second time since I'd met him. I was glad I'd painted my nails.

I looked at my lap for a few seconds, then went on. "We didn't have one of those horrible break ups. I guess I just got fed up. Jess had finally taken a job down at the truck stop pumping gas. Made me refer to him as a 'fuel attendant' when I told my friends what he did. He hadn't had the job long when he woke up one morning and told me he wasn't going in. Didn't say he was sick, just that he wasn't up to it. I stood in the doorway watching him laid up in bed, his hair sticking up in all directions, his scrawny legs poking out from under the sheet blanket.

"Then something inside me snapped. I walked to the kitchen and packed his lunch pail and grabbed his suitcase out of the spare bedroom. I set both of them next to the front door, drug his lazy butt out of bed. 'Jess Harrell,' I said, pointing to the door. 'Over there is a suitcase and a lunch bucket. And by God you're going to pick one of them up and leave with it. And right about now I ain't too concerned which one you take.'"

Well, Brother Debo laughed so hard tears welled up in his green eyes. When he finally settled down, he ran one finger along my jawbone. We sat stone still. I could hear our own breathing. In the background the radio was playing Red Sovine's "Why Baby Why."

Tucking a loose curl behind my ear, Brother Debo started. "You know, Florene, it's not a real popular belief, so I don't preach it from the pulpit. But I don't think divorce is one of the great sins. Seems to me the real sin is the marriage. My sweet Florene, it's the marriage that fails. Divorce is nothing but the aftermath."

Brother Debo looked toward the window above my kitchen sink. "When you think about it," he said, "if God can forgive lying and stealing and even murdering, I don't see why he can't allow for a few failed nuptials."

I stood up then, went to the freezer. I took out an ice tray, pulled the silver lever back until the ice cracked. Brother Debo handed me my glass and then his.

He opened up to me there in my little kitchen. Started telling me about his shut-in wife, how she was practically bed-ridden with some mysterious muscle disorder. At times, he said, she was a powerful burden to him. He mentioned how they were not able to have marital relations. I blushed at that. But I'll tell you, he had a way of telling it, made you think he was a saint for staying with her.

The next Thursday I fried up a chicken, thinking maybe he'd stop by. I swear I wasn't planning on doing anything but having a meal with him. But by six he still hadn't shown up, so I drove over to Haven O' Rest to visit Mama. She was doing okay. Except she thought I was Arvella, her older sister, who's been dead going on twenty years. I played along, though. Seemed to make her happy.

When I drove up that old dog trail that constitutes my driveway, Brother Debo was coming from behind the trailer and making his way up the front steps. His Lincoln wasn't anywhere in sight. Soon as I saw him, I started trembling. Felt like I might pass out. Desire. Desire is a powerful thing, and I had never wanted a man as much as I wanted him at that very minute.

He waited for me, watching me as I made my way out of my car. He put his hand on the small of my back and walked in the door after me. There was fire shooting through his hand. It was traveling through my breasts and settling between my legs.

"Florene," he said, circling me with his arms and leaning me up against the living room wall. "Florene, you're all I think about. It's wrong, I'm not saying it's not, but I dream about you. And when I'm awake I say your name over and over in my head." He tugged at a lock of my hair. "I know the exact color blue your eyes are. And how your brown hair shines gold in the light."

Brother Debo pulled away from me and hooked his fingers through the loops in the waistband of my jeans. I sagged there against the paneling, not trusting my legs to hold me. "The other night at the deacons' meeting," he said, "I couldn't stop thinking about you. Kept smiling like some lovesick fool. Even when we were discussing the bake sale for that little Newton girl who's been stricken with leukemia, I was grinning. I finally had to excuse myself."

I swear I almost called him Brother Debo. Then it occurred to me that two people who were about to do what we were would not be encouraged by religious titles. I called him Ransom for the first time.

He cupped my face in his hands and bent down to kiss me. His mouth was hard on mine. Ransom sucked in my breath like he was trying to pull all the air out of me and into him. I heard my heart beat in my ears.

"Are you sure you want to do this?" he asked, his voice almost a whisper. His body so close to mine I could feel the heat come off it.

Before I could answer, his fingers were tugging at the buttons on my blouse. He pushed the cloth aside and touched the lace on my brassiere.

"I could show you my Grandma CeCe's quilt," I said. "It ain't much, but I could show you." I could feel the color rising in my cheeks. I started talking faster, "It's the only thing she ever made me. She wasn't exactly what you'd call domestic." I pointed down the dark hallway. "It's back in my bedroom."

After I lit a candle on the chest of drawers, I turned down the corner of the quilt. "See," I said, "it ain't much to look at."

"It's beautiful," Ransom said, looking at me instead of the quilt.

I sat on the bed, my three Miss Maizie County banners hanging on the wall above my headboard, the glitter letters almost completely gone from them. I remember thinking I was about to become a great sinner.

Ransom tossed my blouse on the floor, leaned me up against a pillow. He kissed me while he unfastened my brassiere. Undid it real slow and deliberate. It felt like the room was spinning. A clean soapy smell was coming off his body—he hadn't worn the aftershave I remembered from before. I took note of every detail, concentrating so I could replay it all later in my mind.

He was holding my hand to his mouth, running his tongue across my knuckles and into the little grooves between my fingers. He kissed the inside of my wrists and up my arm. When he reached my mouth, he said, "I could do this for a long, long time." The next thing I knew, all my clothes were off. All Ransom's clothes were off. I thought he was beautiful.

Ransom's mouth was on my neck, my thighs, even on my ankles. By the time he reached my breasts, all I could hear was my own breathing, Ransom groaning, and the sound of the attic fan pulling damp air across the room.

It was a powerful feeling, having him inside me. Felt like he could own me if he wanted to, right at that moment. I grabbed onto his arms, feeling his muscles. I remember being surprised that a preacher had any muscles at all since I didn't figure any of them did any kind of physical labor.

Ransom was rocking back and forth inside me, and I was moving with him. All of a sudden, he pulled out of me. He was resting on his elbows above me just gazing into my eyes. I thought I'd die from wanting him.

Soon as he thrust back inside me, I came. My fingers were digging into the flesh on his back, my head thrown back, sweat beading up on my forehead. I had my legs wrapped tight around him, like I was afraid he might bolt and run.

He pulled my hips up to him, propped a pillow underneath. "It'll feel better this way," he said. My head was thrashing from side to side, my hair spread across the gingham pillowcase. Ransom pushed hard inside me. "I've never felt anything this good," he said. It sounded like his voice was somewhere far away.

Damned if I didn't fall in love with him. We started seeing each other every Thursday. Talked on the phone two, three times a day. I never told a soul, and I don't think he did either. Ransom bought me little things: a stuffed cat with glass eyes, some of those strings of colored beads to hang like a curtain in my kitchen doorway, a Ruby and the Romantics album with that song "Our Day Will Come" on it.

I sold Mama's house to Bethel Baptist on a Monday afternoon. I still had on my waitress outfit, but I changed into heels and ratted up my hair where that dumb little hat had smashed it down. We had the closing right there in the church office. Ransom stood up when I walked in, stuck his hand out and shook mine, called me "Miss Huggins." My hand was shaking, but

Ransom stayed steady. Not even the head deacon seemed to notice anything odd about me and Ransom standing hands gripped together, our eyes fixed on one another. I must've signed a hundred papers that day. I didn't get near what I should have for Mama's house, but at the time that didn't seem to matter very much.

We'd been together over two months when one of Ransom's church members saw us together at Haven O' Rest. I was there checking on Mama, and he was doing church visitation. We met up in the hall, walked to his car together. It was a dumb thing to do, but Ransom wanted to talk. It was pitch black inside the car in the parking lot, after nine at night. We thought we were safe. He kissed me hard, slipped his hand up my skirt. We were already to the mouth-breathing part when we heard a woman gasp and the sound of keys hitting the pavement. Turned out the woman was a member of Bethel Baptist. I guess she'd seen Ransom's car and decided to stop by to say hello.

Ransom flew from the driver's seat and ran after the churchgoer. I could hear her high heels click-clacking across the parking lot and Ransom calling out her name. I high-tailed it to my car and headed home. He called me later from a pay phone, said we had to keep a low profile, let this thing blow over. Told me to trust him.

Well, in a place like Maizie County things get spread pretty damn quick. By the next afternoon, I was getting snubbed by both the Freewill and Southern Baptists, and quite a few Nazarenes. Then some cockeyed idiot wheeled Ransom's wife into The Garden of Eating during lunch hour, and she bawled and screamed and damned me to hell. I just have one thing to say about that. For a shut-in, the woman sure had a healthy set of lungs.

When the song leader's wife came in for a rinse down at the Beauty Barn, my friend Cindy said she started spouting off about me and Ransom. The woman claimed Ransom swore to the deacons that there was just the one kiss between us. Said I'd seduced him same as Delilah had Samson. Said I was a test from God and he'd passed it. Though I don't imagine even Ransom could convince them he'd passed with flying colors.

The following Wednesday, somebody stuck a plywood sign up on the Bethel Baptist parking lot. In stick-on letters from the dime store, the sign read, "Sunday's sermon, by Brother Ransom Debo. Adam and Eve. It was the woman who sinned."

Well, that did it for me. I knew right then and there that Ransom Debo wasn't about to come back to me. What love he might have felt was covered up with so much cowardice it might as well have been hate. I drove to the liquor store, bought a bottle of Wild Turkey, and got shit-kicking drunk.

I skipped work on Friday and visited Mama. She was sitting in the recliner by her bed. I knelt down on the brown linoleum floor, rested my head on her lap. She was pulling at her neck, a habit she'd had from way back when.

"Mama," I said. "What in the hell is wrong with me? Everything I do turns out ugly. Failed at everything I ever tried, from Jess Harrell on. Seems like my life peaked when I became Miss Maizie County, and it's been going downhill ever since."

The cold floor was numbing my legs. I started to cry. Mama was running her fingers through my hair.

"Arvella," she said, kind of like a question. She was mistaking me for her dead sister again. Talking to her felt so useless right at that moment that I almost got up and left. But then she picked up the wedding picture she kept on the TV tray beside her chair and said, "I'll tell you a little story if you promise not to tell another soul."

I blew a mouthful of clenched air through my teeth and tried to settle down. "Sure," I said. "I could use a good story right about now."

Mama set the wedding picture back down and started fiddling with my hair again. "You ever notice, Arvella, how babies, when they get to be about two, start pulling off their clothes? Florene did that all the time. Pulled off every stitch." Mama laughed a little. "I'd dress her three, four times a day. I used to think the fabric was itching her or maybe those little socks were pinching her feet."

Mama kicked the recliner back, forcing me to sit up straight. I crawled up on her bed, took off my shoes.

"But then I realized. It wasn't the clothes that bothered Florene. She was just pure was all. Didn't have one sin chalked up against her yet.

"I remember thinking back then—and I was never really a church-going woman—that I would love to be clean enough not to have to hide my sin. I got to thinking about grown folks, how we know to cover ourselves, trying to gloss over the nastiness inside us."

Mama was using her housecoat to polish the dinner ring Daddy had given her on their twenty-fifth wedding anniversary. "Now, none of this was a bolt of lightning. Just an observation, mind you, that I tucked away somewhere inside my head. In fact, I'd forgotten all about it until the summer when I ran off with that truck driver." She looked at me, one eyebrow raised and said. "You didn't know about that, did you, Arvella?"

I shook my head and felt my heart start beating a little faster. "Yep, I left Hamp and Florene. She was only four at the time."

"Lord," I said.

"Well, Arvella," she snapped, "your life ain't exactly spot-free."

I shut up then, sank back in the pillows and let Mama talk.

"I guess I was just fed up. I don't really remember. About three days after we took off, the sorry cuss left me at a truck stop in Albuquerque. Wasn't nothing I could do but call Hamp. He sent me a bus ticket home."

"Well, you know how Hamp was, Arvella. It was weeks before he'd even speak to me. We lived in that cold quiet, with only Florene holding us together."

Over the intercom, a nurse was announcing the end of visiting hours. Mama stopped for a moment, her brow furrowed. I walked over and closed her door so that I wouldn't be run off.

"One day," she said, "I started praying. I asked God to forgive me and let me have Hamp back. I fell into a deep sleep that night—Hamp was still spending nights on the divan—and in a dream it came to me what I had to do."

Mama eased off the recliner, slow as molasses, and walked to the window that somebody had nailed shut years before. "The next night I took a scalding hot bath. My skin was flushed pink when I got out of the tub. I let down my hair—it was to my waist back then—and brushed it till if fell in loose curls. I wanted Hamp to look at me, see that my sin was gone, see how pure I was."

Mama frowned suddenly. She turned and pointed a finger at me. "Arvella," she said, "you promise not to tell anybody. I'd hate to have folks talking behind my back."

I was sitting on the edge of the bed facing Mama, my elbow on my knee and my chin in my hand. "I promise," I said, barely above a whisper.

Mama had pulled a handkerchief from her housecoat and was twisting it around her index finger. "I stood naked in front of Hamp, right under the ceiling light, and called out his name. He stirred some and finally sat up. I dropped my arms to my side, lowered my head. Hamp understood. He scooped me up in his arms and carried me to bed. Hamp never slept on the divan again.

"Of course what you've got to understand, Arvella, is that exposing myself was a show of repentance, an outward act, like, say, baptism. Getting Hamp back was just the bonus."

Mama was losing momentum. I guided her to the bed and pulled the slippers off her feet. "I figure it this way, if folks were willing to show each other what dirt or sparkle rested beneath their clothes, it'd be a hell of a lot easier to tell who was pure and who wasn't. The simple fact is this, Arvella, folks don't get naked near enough."

I spent most of Saturday thinking about what Mama said.

Sunday morning the sun came up, a bright orange dot in the sky, spilling light across the steeple on Bethel Baptist's rooftop. A crowd had gathered for Ransom's newest sermon. I could hear the organ music from all the way over at Mama's house, where I'd slipped in through the back door just after Sunday school ended. Outside, the overflow traffic had parked in her yard, a pickup had crushed her crepe myrtle.

I figured there wasn't more than thirty- or forty-five minutes worth of preaching left in Ransom. But he surprised me; I'll give him that. It was past noon when the invitation started up. Right about then I climbed up on the divan and pushed back my mom's velvet curtains. All these remnants of my mom still in place. The sun felt warm on my naked breasts. I leaned up against the plate glass window, listening to the last chords of "Are You Washed in the Blood?" fade away, just waiting for church to let out.

THE END

ACKNOWLEDGEMENTS

Versions of the majority of the stories in this book were first published in *Do South* magazine. Additionally, "She'll Be Back," "Calling Out the Moon," "On the Eve of the Eve of the End of the World," and "Carry Me Over" were subsequently published in *Deep South* magazine. "Miss Maizie County's Public Disgrace" was first published in the *Showoff Anthology*. "Past the End of Everything" was also in *Kindred, Family Anthology*; "Up on Piney Mountain" in *Carrying Fire, Women's Anthology*; and "As Long as You Remember" in *Beneath Strange Stars Anthology*.

GRATITUDE

Anita Paddock inspired and encouraged me as a new writer, praising me when I needed it most. I can never repay her, but I will always keep trying. To my writer friends, L.P., Gwen, Carla, Marcus, Tom, and Dixie, thank you for your considerable help with *Early Morning in the Land of Dreams*.

My life as a short story writer blossomed when I was working with *Do South* magazine. I'm thankful for that, and for Catherine, who gave me the chance. To Debbie, owner of Chapters on Main, thank you for believing I could teach writing at your beautiful store. I would never have tried without you.

To the Arkansas Arts Council, I'm grateful for the Fellowship Award for Short Fiction. That award helped me believe I had something important to say.

Finally, to my friends and my sweet family near and far, thank you for all that you do and all that you are. You are my heart.

BIOGRAPHICAL NOTE

Marla Cantrell is the award-winning writer of more than 100 published short stories. She's also a freelance journalist with work that has appeared in *Woman's World*, *Huffington Post*, *AY* magazine, *Entertainment Fort Smith*, *The Fort Report*, *Arkansas Outdoors*, *Do South* magazine, and *Arkansas Money and Politics*.

Marla is the winner of the Arkansas Arts Council Fellowship Award in Short Fiction, the owner of Telephee Press, a writing coach and editor, and the director of the Alma Public Library in Arkansas. You can read more about her at marlacantrell.com.

Made in USA - Crawfordsville, IN
94297_9781735725505
10.14.2020 1554